THE MISSING TREASURE HUNTER

A Shay Hamilton, Lori Mysek, and Winslow Doyle Mystery

David Francis Curran

ISBN-13: 978-1-881417-75-0
ISBN-10: 1-881417-75-1

Cover design by: David Francis Curran

CHAPTER 1: I-90

NOTE: Chapters are presented in the best way to tell the story. Consequently, they are not arranged linearly. Please note the timeline of each chapter to see if its events occur before or after the previous chapter.

•

June 28, 2022: Noon

Shay Hamilton was just twenty-seven years old when he met Lori Mysek in a truly unexpected manner.

Driving East in the direction of Deer Lodge on I-90, he had just passed Drummond and was now on a curving stretch of road heading home.

A Celtic Woman CD filled the cab with music, loud enough to be heard over the wind that rushed in through the open windows of his air-conditioner-less, light-blue Chevy Silverado.

The aspen and willow were green, and the Clark Fork River gleamed in the sun. Stony bluffs climbed to the south with beards of larch, lodgepole and subalpine fir on the slopes beneath them. The air smelled, as it always did, of a medley of pines. Cattle and horses roamed the grassy hills, between the islands of trees on the north side of the highway. Shay felt glad to be alive. Fishing season was open, and Shay began to imagine casting one of the elk-hair Parachute Adams he'd tied the night before.

Thinking of fly-fishing was better than thinking about the two adjustable room heaters in the twenty-unit motel he'd inherited from his uncle, which didn't seem to be able to put out any heat at all. Luckily, the two's air-conditioner functions worked. Good heater/air conditioners ran about $1,000 apiece.

He'd have to replace both before too long. He already had one mortgage on the motel. How he was going to replace the units he did not know. His thoughts led to getting another source of income, and that thought led to the Private Investigator certificate he had recently earned from an online school. Becoming a detective was something he'd been thinking of since he read 'Gumshoe Reflections in a Private Eye, 'a book by Josiah Thompson. Shay had read the book while a student in Florida, but the problem was that in Montana, unless you were a law enforcement officer, you had to apprentice for a few years with a licensed Private Investigator to get a license.

His framed private-investigator certificate hung in the office behind the main desk. The difficulty was finding someone he could actually work with to get a license.

One company in Butte was willing to let him have an apprenticeship, a non-paid apprenticeship, but with running his motel he wasn't sure he could swing being away as much as that job would require. The company had specifically said he would be doing surveillance work and might be on stakeouts for twenty-four hours at a time.

Shay decided to focus on something else.

Except for the occasional Semi headed toward Missoula in the other lane, he'd seen little traffic, and for some time, he hadn't seen a vehicle ahead of him. As he rounded a curve, a flashing orange sign informed him there was construction ahead, and that the left lane was closed.

He had been traveling at the allowed speed limit on much of I-90—eighty miles per hour—but now a portable sign ahead read 35 MPH for the construction area.

As he slowed, the highway straightened. Shay began to catch up to a brown Ford Explorer, seeming to drive more slowly than necessary. Ahead, the two lanes became a single lane between a line of orange cones and the right lane's shoulder. The cones marked the boundary of the left passing lane, now a pile of broken pavement.

Hanging back about one hundred yards behind the Explorer in the single lane of the construction area, Shay was surprised when the brake lights flashed, and the vehicle swerved abruptly onto the shoulder.

No sooner did it lurch off the highway, than it lurched back.

Instinctively, Shay pressed down on his brake. Something was wrong.

The brake lights flashed again, and once more the vehicle lurched onto the shoulder, but this time the brake lights stayed on. The Explorer came to an abrupt stop with its rear end protruding into the driving lane.

Normally, Shay would have moved into the left lane to give the perhaps drunken driver as much room as possible, but due to the construction, that wasn't an option.

Some fifty yards from the Explorer, Shay slowed even more and began to edge as far to the left as he could, while avoiding the orange cones.

By the time he reached the SUV, he was moving at a crawl. Luckily, there were no other vehicles behind him.

He was about forty feet from the rear end of the Explorer when the passenger door flew open.

A slim woman dressed in a short-sleeved, blue waitress uniform, just barely taller than the top of the SUV, jumped out of the passenger seat. A moment later, a dark-haired man emerged from the driver's side door.

Shay hit his brakes hard.

"God damn you, Lori," the man shouted. He was a big man, his shoulders were visible above the top of the SUV. The man had to be at least six feet tall, a little taller than Shay.

Whirling her bare right arm, the woman tossed something high in the air.

Shay's eyes followed the object, which glinted in the sun as it arched over the guard rail and the brush closest to the highway toward the train tracks that Shay knew ran between the highway and the river.

The man was now lurching toward the front of the SUV. His gait was hampered by a brace on his right leg, which embraced him from a twisted foot to just below his knee.

"You god-damn whore," he was shouting as he rounded the front of the vehicle.

The woman backed toward the rear of the vehicle, keeping an eye on the man as she did so.

Shay had come to a complete stop.

Not looking where she was going, the woman backed right into the side of his truck. Startled, she turned to stare at Shay. She had a curly mop of light-brown hair streaked with blonde, and her blue eyes looked at Shay like a deer caught in headlights.

Then, to Shay's surprise, she stuck out her thumb. There was a desperate look in her eyes.

Past her, the furious-looking man rounded the front of the truck.

Shay's stomach seemed to sink. A rush of adrenaline set his heart racing. A memory that brought back fear tried to surface in his mind, but there was no time for that.

Shay reached over and unlocked the passenger door. He didn't need to say anything. The girl, for she seemed more of a girl than a woman, opened the door and jumped into the truck.

Shay could see the crippled man veering toward them. The man had a look of rage in his eyes like Shay had rarely seen.

"Go," the girl urged.

The man lurched forward and for a moment his face hung within a foot of the passenger window. His right arm moved as if to grab the door handle.

Shay stepped on the gas.

In the rearview mirror, Shay saw the man, who had been reaching for the door handle, fall.

"Thank you," the girl said, trying to catch her breath.

"You're welcome," Shay said. "Are you alright?"

"What do you think?" she laughed, shaking her head nervously. She looked as if she were in shock.

"Sorry, is there someplace I can take you?"

"Can you give me a minute to think?" she replied.

"Sure," Shay said as kindly as he could.

Shay's heart was still racing. He had thought little about what he was doing. But now the situation hit him. The anger in the man's countenance brought back an unwanted memory. Houlihan. Shay had never even learned his first name, a muscle-bound, black-haired, towering bully who Shay'd caught with Shay's then wife, Annelle, in their bed in their home. A man who'd had the nerve to threaten Shay when Shay had confronted them.

Who was this woman he had just let into his car? Would the man give chase? Was she a thief, or a crook, or a whore as the man had labeled her?

From the corner of his eye, he saw her lift a small black purse that he had not realized she was carrying in her left hand. She opened the purse and began rummaging inside.

Shay's first thought was that she was about to do some sort of drugs, and he wondered what he would do if she suddenly lit up a meth pipe in his truck.

Almost confirming his fear, she produced a small, black, cloth bag from the purse. Opening the strings on the bag, she took out two thumb-sized stones, one pink and the other an almost-transparent pale green. She put the bag back in the purse and put one stone in her free hand. She put the purse down, then she held both stones in her fists with her palms up.

Curious to the point of not being able to help himself, Shay said, "You're not going to hit me with those stones, are you?"

The girl shook her head slightly, and an almost smile crossed her lips. "I'm just holding them. Stones have energies and they can absorb energy. I'm just using these two to calm down."

"I'm Shay Hamilton, by the way," Shay said.

"Of Hamilton's Hurricane Motel? she asked.

'You've heard of it?" Shay asked surprised.

She shook her head again. "It's on the door of your truck."

"Oh, right."

"I'm Lori... Lori Mysek."

They drove in silence; Shay checked the rearview mirror every few seconds.

"Would that man try to follow, you think?" Shay finally asked. The Explorer was a few minutes behind them now, but Shay had a vision of the man suddenly coming up behind them and ramming the rear of his truck.

"He's my husband, Victor." Lori said. She was looking at the stones in her hand, as if she could see down into them. "He would definitely smash right into you, but I think we're safe. I'm pretty sure I threw his keys far enough down into the brush by the railroad tracks that it will take him a while to find them." She thought for a moment. "Do you have a room for me at your motel? I don't think it's safe for me back at my apartment."

Shay considered the idea. If Lori had noticed the motel's logo on the side of the truck, her husband might have also.

"We do, and I can give you the room at the very end of the motel, just in case your husband saw the sign, too, and comes looking for you."

"That would be great," she said. "Victor will probably go back to my apartment first, but he'll come looking for you if he noticed the sign, and since you were driving away with me, it's most likely he did."

"I will deal with him if he shows up," Shay said.

"I really appreciate this," she said, and then a moment later, "I'd have to pay you later, if that's okay. I hide my tips in a honey jar and don't have much with me."

"I'll trust you," Shay said. He wondered if he'd actually get paid. The fact that she was pretty didn't make her honest, something he'd learned the hard way, but he could afford the loss of one night's room rent, or even a few. Though it was the beginning of the summer season, a few rooms would be empty. "I take it you don't live with your husband?"

"Him? Never! He's been in prison for the last five years."

She didn't offer more, and Shay found himself saying, "I take it, it wasn't a pleasant reunion?"

For some time, Lori was quiet. She wiped a tear from her eye and looked out the front window. To Shay, her bright eyes and pretty face should have belonged to a happier woman. She was pretty enough to get any man she wanted, and though the man he had caught a glimpse of could be considered handsome, he obviously had a bad temper.

"I've been trying to get a divorce from him for years now. He got out of prison yesterday and appeared at my door a few hours ago.

"He told me he had a lawyer in Butte who he wanted to go over the divorce papers with before he signed them. He told me he needed me to come along to agree to any changes. That's how he got me into his car."

Lori paused as if to compose herself.

"So, we are on the road, and he starts saying he wants to get back together. I told him no. He kept going on and on. I said I wanted out of the car. He sped up. Finally, I told him I was pregnant. I am, and it is not his. There were no conjugal visits at the prison. He blew up. He started pounding the ceiling, the window, and the steering wheel with his hands. I grabbed the steering wheel. He hit the brakes as we veered onto the shoulder. He grabbed the wheel away like a madman.

"Terrified, I let him have the wheel, but then I thought what the hell and I grabbed it back. We hit the shoulder again. I leaned over, grabbed the key, and shut off the engine. I got his keys free and got my door open.

"I was about to start running down the highway when you showed up. With his leg in a brace, I didn't think he could catch me if I ran."

Shay only vaguely heard what Lori said after she admitted that she was pregnant by another man. His memory leaped back to Annelle, his wife. He'd come home to their Florida apartment early, as the air-conditioning unit had broken at the humanities building, and classes had been canceled for the day.

He'd called her name when he got home, but there had been no reply, and he thought she might be out. When he had gone to their bedroom to change, he found them, Annelle and Houlihan. Neither of them noticed him for a while. Annelle had been more vocal in her pleasure than he ever remembered her being with him.

But Lori's situation was entirely different. From what he saw of her husband, he couldn't blame her for wanting to get away from him.

"You know, thinking about it, are you sure it wouldn't be safer for me to take you somewhere else?" Shay asked. "I can drive you to Butte. I'm sure you can find a room there," Shay said.

"I don't have any money to pay for a regular motel room," she replied quietly after a moment.

"What about the father of your unborn baby? Can you go to him?"

"We broke up when he found out I'm pregnant."

Shay glanced at her. She looked devastated. A tear ran down her cheek.

"You can stay as long as you need to," Shay said.

"Thank you," Lori said. "But what will we do it he comes around?"

"Yeah, I remember the girl. She was your wife? I dropped her off at the Holiday Inn in Butte," Shay said.

Lori smiled.

CHAPTER 2: VICTOR

June 28, 2022: 11:49 a.m.

Victor Bleché's heart beat steadily in his chest as he looked over at his wife, Lori. He watched her stare out the passenger side window. She refused to look at him. All he had thought about during his last months in prison was getting back with her.

She had not met him at the prison to bring him home. She had not visited him in almost five years, but he had hoped, when he knocked on her door with the bouquet of roses in his hands, she might have remembered how they felt about each other before he had gone to prison. He hoped that she might have opened her arms and welcomed him with a hug.

Instead, she had asked without a hint of tenderness, "Did you sign the divorce papers?"

So, he had tricked her, telling her that he had a lawyer in Butte that wanted to go over the papers, and then he'd sign, and then, she had willingly gotten into his car.

His friend, Bozo (for Bozo the Clown), the nickname inmates had given John Cristy Feldor, his cellmate in Deer Lodge prison, had warned him how she might react. Bozo's wife had tried to leave him when Bozo was in for the first time. Bozo told Victor about the cabin he had built in the woods on an acre of land he'd purchased. He had taken his wife there to change his wife's mind.

"There's no street names. And it wasn't easy to find in the first place," Bozo had said.

He'd given Victor general directions, but it had been years

since Bozo had been to the cabin. Logging in the area had changed some of the landmarks Bozo had described.

So, Victor had combed the wilderness areas between Drummond and Deer Lodge. Finally, he found the one-room cabin on an overgrown dirt track, far off the main forest road.

The cabin was in good shape, despite not having been used in years.

"You need to stock it with provisions for a month. No. Two months," the lean rail of a man who had been a circus clown said, sitting on the lower bunk beside Victor. It wasn't just his having been a circus clown that had earned Bozo his name. It wasn't his balding head with long red hair on the sides. It wasn't his perpetually sad face, either. Bozo had a rep. If you messed with Bozo the Clown, you'd die laughing.

So, Victor had stocked the cabin. It was remote enough that no one had noticed his goings and comings. All he had to do now was get Lori there.

"You gotta treat her right," Bozo had warned. "You can't force her into loving you. That was my mistake." That was why Bozo was in prison for life. His wife had been tortured to death in that cabin.

Victor had nodded in agreement, but he knew he'd have to contain the anger he felt for such a long time over Lori abandoning him and asking for a divorce.

However, sometimes in his cell, Victor felt so alone. All he could think of was Lori, and how, way back when, she had made him feel loved just by smiling at him.

.

"I really don't want a divorce, you know?" Victor said, with as much feeling as he could put into the words as they drove ostensibly to Butte.

Lori seemed to flinch. She still stared out the window and didn't look at him.

"I would think of you in prison. Not just about sex, but in a good way. About how it was when we were first married. How we could just be together and be happy just being together." He glanced at her to see how she'd react.

Lori turned toward him. She seemed to pull herself together like a pitcher winding up to throw a 100-mph-plus fastball. She spoke slowly and evenly. "I do want a divorce. It is the only thing I want from you, then I would prefer never seeing you again..." She paused for a moment and caught her breath. "So, if you think some little speech is going to change my mind, you can forget it."

Victor was silent as his eyes blurred with rage. In the back of his mind, he knew he should hold off telling her his plan, but it was as if his anger was pushing it out.

"Well, you are in for a little surprise. We are not going to see a lawyer in Butte. I have a cabin in the wilderness. I am taking you there, and I am going to keep you there, until you learn to love me again."

When he glanced at her, her face was a stone mask. She was silent for a long-drawn-out moment, and then she again spoke calmly, "Well, then you'd better know I'm pregnant, and for obvious reasons, it's not yours."

Victor felt his face burn, his heart pound. In that instant, if he hadn't been driving, he might have torn her to pieces.

"Who the hell is this guy?" he asked, fighting to control himself and speak as calmly as he could, thinking as he did so, whoever he is, I'll kill him.

His hands were vice-tight on the steering wheel. His view of the construction zone they were driving through reddened, as if in a bloody mist. For a moment, everything in his view burst into flames, reminding him of the last time he'd experienced that level of rage.

Suddenly, he could smell gasoline. He knew he was imagining it. He fought to escape the smell and the vision. Moments later, he found himself pounding the steering wheel, pounding the dash.

As he fought that vision of flames, Lori grabbed the

steering wheel, and they went onto the shoulder for the first time.

He wrenched the steering wheel away from her and got the Explorer back on the road.

"Stay calm," he told himself.

Lori grabbed the wheel again, this time with two hands.

They were on the shoulder again, and he had to hit the brake to avoid hitting the guard rail. This time she went for the keys. She turned the engine off, pulled the ignition key, opened the passenger door, and then she jumped out.

He threw open his door, got his feet out the door and was standing when he saw the arc of her arm, and the keys flying up high in the air on the other side of the car. He watched the keys glint in the sun as they flew over the guardrail, and he cried out, voicing his rage like a tornado escaping from his lungs.

There was a Blue Chevy pickup coming close in the driving lane, which meant that Lori would not be able to go around the back of the Explorer. Victor went as fast as he could around the front, but his leg brace slowed him like a heavy weight, and by the time he was around the front, she was by the rear bumper. The pickup came to a stop.

It seemed almost as if he was moving in slow motion. Lori stuck her thumb out. Victor watched the driver of the truck lean over toward the passenger door. If he lets her in…

Somehow, gaining ground, He watched Lori open the door of the pickup and get in. If he could only reach the door before it closed.

She slammed the door just before he could grab it. The engine roared. Victor lurched for the door handle. The pickup's tires squealed. Victor fell as the pickup took off, spraying road grit in Victor's face. Victor screamed.

He saw the words on the side of the truck. Hamilton's Hurricane Motel. They burned into his mind.

The name on the truck stayed with him as he struggled over the guardrail and down the bank. The name stayed with him as he pushed the brush around by the railroad tracks, trying to find his keys. That guy would pay for this someday.

CHAPTER 3: SHAY

June 28, 2022: 12:12 p.m.

Shay looked over at Lori with sympathy. He had picked her up, and now he was responsible for her.

Would it be better to take her to Butte and pay for a motel room? He'd have to find a motel that had a room, and it could be expensive if he agreed to pay for a room for the indefinite period if it took her a while to find another place to live, and he had no assurance she'd pay him back.

On the other hand, if he put her up in his motel, it would cost him nothing. He seemed to always have an empty room available. The problem was the motel logo on the side of the truck.

He really couldn't afford to pay for her to be somewhere else. He realized the only reason he'd thought of the idea was because he was nervous about the possibility of confronting her husband if he did come looking for her.

"Cheer up. You are welcome to stay as long as you need to," he assured her again as he glanced over at her.

She wiped her eyes and looked at him. Her big eyes bored into his. "Thank you," she said. "Victor, when I met him, was a really nice guy, but isn't the same person I married. Now, he scares me."

Shay thought for a bit, then said, "I'm sorry that happened to you."

.

Shay pulled off I-90 and turned left at the end of the exit ramp. The motel was a minute's drive away through grassy hillsides and a smattering of pine forest.

As Shay bypassed the entrance by the office, and drove toward the far entrance of the parking lot, Lori got a view of the white, sprawling motel.

"Wow, this is nice," Lori said.

To Shay, the place was ordinary. Yes, he kept the paint up on the white walls and the Adirondack chairs in front of each unit. The only unpainted thing was the split-rail fence he'd made himself and put in around the parking area. The grass was green and almost in need of cutting already, but he guessed the place did have a quaint charm.

Shay took the next turn and slowed as he entered the parking lot through the back entrance.

"I'm putting you in this end unit." he said, pointing at the door with a big #20 on it. It isn't that popular as it doesn't have parking right in front of it. It's the best hiding spot we have."

He turned to her, and said firmly, "But this is important! If you want to stay here, you need to stay in your room. We'll figure out something concerning food, and that kind of stuff, but I don't want problems, and that is what we'll have if your husband comes along and sees you."

"Thank you," Lori said.

"We need to stop at the office to get you a key," Shay said.

Shortly after, Shay pulled in front of the larger structure with its little neon sign reading 'Office. 'Next to the office was a metal V-shaped tower which held the 'Hamilton's Hurricane Motel' sign. Beneath that sign was another neon sign, which blinked the word 'Vacancy.'

The ' no' in front of the vacancy had rarely been lit since he'd taken over for his deceased uncle two years before.

"Come on in, and I'll get you sorted with a key," Shay said.

As Lori stepped inside, Shay watched her take in the bright white walls, the modern main desk and the tall, coffee-skinned woman with an Afro hairdo who sat behind it. An open door behind the main desk led to what looked like a tiny office. Flowers had been placed on three stands along the walls. Another door loomed to the far left of the desk. Several plaques were mounted on the wall behind the desk next to the office door.

The woman behind the desk stood.

A look of surprise crossed Lori's face.

Issy, at over six feet tall, had that effect on people. Isadora Wint, Shay's assistant, smiled at the two of them with her dark brown eyes.

"Hi, Boss," Issy greeted him. Issy had come from Jamaica, the island, not Queens County. Thin as a rail, and sporting that halo of black and curly hair, to Shay she was a treasure. She cleaned the rooms, took reservations, manned the office when he was gone, and so many other things Shay couldn't name them all. Shay did not know if Issy was legally in the country, but he chose to ignore the question. Because her mother had been what they called in her neighborhood in Jamaica, deaf and dumb, Issy could even sign and read lips.

"Do we have a guest?" Issy asked as she took in Lori.

Shay turned and looked back at Lori. The girl—for she looked so young, he kept thinking of her as more of a girl than a woman—looked defeated.

A sudden feeling of sympathy touched him. This girl had nothing, and she was forced now into taking charity.

"Number 20, our finest suite for my guest..." and then mouthed silently, "...if anyone comes looking for her, she is NOT here."

Issy nodded that she understood.

"Lori Mysek," Shay continued, this is Issy Wint, my assistant manager, handywoman, etc."

"Don't forget housekeeper, a more pleasant term for toilet scrubber," Issy said. "He give me the shitty jobs too."

Lori smiled. "Nice to meet you!" She held out her hand, and Issy shook it.

"Can you get her squared away, Issy? I've got to get the

toilet in my truck into unit four."

"I take care of her, boss."

Shay had turned to go but turned back. "Did you find anyone to take Eudora's place?" Shay asked. Eudora, a hardworking room cleaner, had quit two days before to work in Missoula, where she lived.

"Been looking. Not many want come all the way out here."

Shay smiled. When he had interviewed Issy, who had a masters in computer science, she spoke in perfect English with impeccable diction. He suspected she had applied for a job at his out-of-the-way motel, because she was not in this country legally.

But, after hiring her, when she first lapsed into her Jamaican prosody, he'd asked her about it.

"Speaking this way, just be comfortable for me, boss," she'd said, then added, "If that is a problem for you, Mr. Hamilton, I can make sure I always speak the king's English."

Shay thought for a moment, then smiled. "There don't be no king here. You don't be having to speak his language," he'd replied.

Issy laughed.

They'd quickly became friends, and Issy was proving to be invaluable.

CHAPTER 4: LORI

June 28, 2022: 12:41 p.m.

Lori almost felt relief as the lobby door swung shut behind Shay as he went to take care of the toilet. There was no point in objecting to the charity she was being offered. She had no choice, but she did feel embarrassed. She would pay this man back.

She took in the office, which was painted in the same white as the outside of the units. It was spotless. The bouquets of mixed flowers sitting on stands by a window near the door and on stands along the wall gave the place charm. Their scent filled the little office.

"Number twenty be a very nice room with a view," Issy offered.

"I'm sure it will be fine," Lori said.

Moments later, Lori followed Issy out the office door. As they walked to the far end of the motel, Lori felt relieved she'd be as far away from anyone visiting the office as possible.

Issy opened the door with a key card and then handed the card to Lori.

Lori hadn't known what to expect, but as they stepped inside, she was pleasantly surprised. Sun coming in the glass sliding doors on the back wall filled the room with light. The room was typical with a bed, a nightstand, a low dresser with a mirror, a television, and a microwave oven, but with the mountain view out the sliding doors, it seemed luxurious and cheerful.

"This is beautiful," Lori said. She began to cry again.

"You been crying, girl? Be everything alright?"

Lori shook her head.

"You tell Issy. Telling can make you better."

CHAPTER 5: SHAY

June 28, 2022: 1:24 p.m.

Shay lived in a large apartment attached to the motel office. He'd washed up in #4 after replacing the toilet and returned to the office. By the time he was done, it was nearly five and Issy would be leaving for the day. Her home, a double-wide belonging to Shay, sat about a city block away from the motel.

"It be nice you're doing for that poor girl," Issy said as he walked in.

"We just have to hope her husband doesn't show up. If he does come looking for her, we'll need to convince him she is not here," Shay said.

"He be a very very bad man."

Shay looked up from the pile of mail he was looking at. "So, you talked to her already?"

Issy nodded.

At first, Issy's nosing into the affairs of their guests had bothered Shay, but over time it seemed she had a knack for solving some of the guests 'personal problems, which had resulted in return visitors.

"She has more than one problem. She's pregnant," Shay said. "And the guy who got her pregnant broke up with her. Said he loved her and then, apparently, dumped her."

He thought of his own life. He'd loved Annelle with his whole heart, and even after the two years that now separated them, he still felt the hurt of her betrayal. Deep down he knew he still loved her and that was the reason it still hurt. Her birthday was in April, and he had sat by the phone in his apartment, torn between calling her and just trying harder to let her go.

"That be bad enough, but the man she love and marry, he be not the same man anymore," Issy said.

Shay looked at Issy again. "She told me that. What exactly does it mean?"

Issy kept her large iPad near her at all times. It had a case and a keyboard. She brought it over and held it out to him. "At first she love him very much, but then he do this stupid thing."

On the screen was a newspaper article. It was dated April 23, 2017.

Mechanic arrested for private airport fire.

A 22-year-old Drummond Man, Victor Bleché, was arrested yesterday afternoon for arson. The young man, married with no children, admitted to setting the fire, so that he could be the first volunteer firefighter on the scene. The fire destroyed four private planes and the hangar they were stored in. Damage estimates are close to over four million dollars. Bleché, who worked at the hangar as a mechanic, admitted starting the fire. He said that he had not realized it would get so out of hand.

"She didn't just fall out of love with him, because he made a really stupid mistake, did she?" Shay asked.

"No," Issy shook her head.

"What happened?"

"He changed. When she first visit him at the prison, men picked on him. They said things about her. They asked her to do dirty things right in front of him. He did nothing. She was embarrassed, but she loved him and keep going back.

"But, then a man broke his leg."

Shay looked at Issy inquiringly.

"The next time she went to visit him, he was in the hospital. He told her a barbell fell on his leg in the gym, but she could tell he was lying. She could see real fear in his eyes. He cried in her arms. She told me, the strong man she loved seemed to be hiding somewhere.

"She visited him three times in that first week he was in

the hospital. The next week he was still in the hospital, but he was no longer crying. His eyes were empty. She said it frightened her, because it seemed the man she married was going away."

Issy paused and looked off. A tear ran down her cheek.

"There be a big change the next time she visit. He was back in the visiting room. His leg had been put into a special brace, because the bone would not heal right, but now, she said, the other men shied away from him—like they were afraid of him.

"She said his eyes were different. There was no fear in them now, but there was also no longer any light. She said she'd never seen eyes so cold.

"On subsequent visits, he be asking her to bring things. Like girlie magazines. She was embarrassed and didn't want to do this, because they searched her before she was allowed into the prison. When she told him, 'no,' he exploded and threatened her.

"She didn't want to visit hm anymore, but she still went. However, now on every visit, he'd get mad about something. She skipped a visit.

"He was so furious the next time she did go, it terrified her. The men were not restrained in the visiting room. The guards actually had to pull him away from her. She stopped going, because she was too afraid to go back.

"After a year, she sent divorce papers. Of course, he wouldn't sign them."

Shay was wondering why the men in the visiting room went from bullying the man to acting afraid of him. The question stirred a memory. It was something Shay read in a newspaper.

"Do you know when this happened? When he broke his leg?"

"He confessed, so he didn't have a trial. They gave him five years. I believe his leg was broken the first month he was there."

Based on what Issy had found out from Lori, Shay could understand Lori wanting to find someone else, but the change in the other prisoners 'attitude intrigued him.

After Issy said goodbye for the day, Shay looked online for any news concerning the prison in the months after Victor was arrested. He found one thing. Slightly less than a month after Victor went into the prison, this article appeared:

Authorities investigating unexplained death.

Authorities at Deer Lodge prison are investigating the death of thirty-seven-year-old Anson Smith, whose body was found in the laundry room, suffering from severe burns. Smith, who worked in the laundry room, had been missing from his cell. A search had been made and his body discovered. An autopsy has been scheduled at the state crime lab in Missoula.

If this Anson had broken Victor's leg and Victor had retaliated by burning the man alive, that might explain a dramatic change in Victor's behavior.

Shay had had a friend, Jeffery Small, who had fought in Afghanistan. He had come back broken and angry. When Shay had visited him, Shay didn't recognize the same man.

Was it possible that Lori's Victor had killed the man who maimed him in Deer Lodge, and that the murder had changed him?

If that was the case, it would certainly explain why Lori would fear the man.

It also occurred to Shay that this Victor might be someone who would not take Shay's driving off with his estranged wife, well, and that the man, who Shay had certainly pissed off, was very likely a killer.

As Shay got into bed that night, he decided he needed to find out more about the man. He laughed to himself, thinking his private investigator course was finally going to pay off. He knew exactly where to start.

CHAPTER 6: VICTOR

June 28, 2022: 1:12 p.m.

When Victor found the keys, he turned and looked up toward his Ford Explorer. The lights of a highway patrol car were flashing behind it. Victor cringed.

"Officer," Victor said, after he climbed over the guard rail and was close enough to the officer who was inspecting the front license plate for the man to hear.

"Is this your vehicle, sir?" the cop asked.

"Yes, sir," Victor said. He knew if the cop found out he was an ex-con; it might not go easy for him.

With one look at the Explorer, he realized his rear end was sticking out into the single driving lane. Victor decided the best course of action was to tell at least part of the truth.

"My wife got mad, said to let her out. When I didn't, she grabbed the wheel and ran us off the road."

"Where is your wife now, sir?"

"Somebody stopped and gave her a ride. She took the keys when we stopped. And threw them down the bank. I just found them." Victor held the keys up.

The cop looked Victor up and down. Obviously checking for blood, or other signs there had been a struggle, or for signs Victor was drunk.

"License and registration," the cop said.

.

"I'll wait and let you pull out first. Drive Carefully," was all the cop said when he came back from his vehicle and handed Victor his license and registration.

"I will, Officer," Victor said pleasantly, but Victor was seething inside. He wanted a chance to think.

Victor started his Explorer, but then, suddenly, the cop's siren and lights went on. Victor hit the brakes. The cop car eased past him and sped down the highway.

Victor tried to decide what to do. He thought that the most likely thing Lori would do would be to try to get back to her apartment. She probably would have asked the guy who picked her up to take her there.

No traffic was coming from either direction. The only thing separating the East bound and West Bound lanes were traffic cones. Victor pulled a U-turn and headed back toward Drummond.

.

Victor parked in the same spot he had parked in when he had picked up Lori earlier. Now the one other car that had been there earlier was gone. Lori's building was a two-story white box. Her apartment was on the second floor on his right side. He scanned the windows of the apartment but couldn't see any sign she might be inside.

The front door was not locked. He entered the vestibule and climbed the stairs to the second floor. Pressing his ear to her door, he listened but heard no sounds from inside.

The hallway was quiet. On his earlier visit, he had heard a radio playing. That radio was no longer playing. There was a good chance no one was in the building. He thought of Lori hiding inside, and the red mist began to swirl behind his eyes.

Taking a few steps back from the door, he charged it. The flimsy door broke open with a crash. He held still. Listened. There were no sounds to be heard in the hallway. No sounds in the building at all. It did not mean that someone wasn't calling 911 right then and there. He had to hurry.

The apartment consisted of a tiny kitchen, a living room/ dining room, a bedroom, and bathroom. He looked in the bedroom closet and the one by the bathroom. He looked under her bed.

Her address book was in the top drawer of the desk in the bedroom.

Putting the address book in his shirt pocket, he decided to leave her a little message. He started by sweeping her desk lamp off the desk and into the wall. The green glass shade shattered along with the lightbulb, making a tinkling-crunching sound. It was music to Victor's ears.

He walked around the apartment breaking things. He saved the bedroom for last.

Taking his knife out, he pulled back the blankets and sheets, intending to cut down into the mattress, but then he had a better idea. Loosening his belt, he lowered his pants and left a dark surprise in the middle of his wife's bed, which he then covered with her blankets and sheets. On the wall above her bed there was a framed diploma. Victor laughed. It was for the course she took in private investigation. Without thinking, he took it into his right hand and sailed it Frisbee-like at the bedroom window. The framed diploma hit the glass between the lilac curtains. The glass splintered with a loud crack. The upper part of the window's glass slid out of its frame and fell like a guillotine, resulting in a loud tinkling crash.

Wow!

A squirrel barked at him from a tree right outside the window. Victor laughed.

A moment later, Victor caught himself. Someone might have heard or seen the frame flying out the window. It was time to leave.

Suddenly, a noise from the hallway stopped him in his tracks. Victor listened. There were no other sounds for a few moments, and then, a door closed.

CHAPTER 7:
WINSLOW DOYLE

June 28, 2022: 2:26 p.m.

Broad-shouldered, clean-shaven, Deputy Sheriff Winslow Doyle at six foot two looked every bit the western lawman as he approached the second-story apartment door in Drummond.

The deaf woman who had reported a possible break-in had seemed extremely frightened to the dispatcher and the Sheriff had called Winslow who, although a part-time deputy, was in the area.

The door of the apartment did not seem to be closed properly. Winslow touched the door, and it eased open an inch. A glance at the door frame showed someone had broken in, probably by kicking in the door.

Suddenly, he heard a sound from inside the apartment. There was a scraping and then a tinkling sound like a piece of glass falling.

Removing his Raging Bull revolver in .454 Casull from its holster, Winslow held it in front of him as he put his left hand on the door, ready to push it all the way open.

Before he could open the door, there was a sound of a door opening below. Glancing down, he saw a tiny figure who at first, he thought was a young teen, but then realized it was a gray-haired woman in a pink bathrobe. The woman looked up at him. Her light-blue eyes were wide with fear.

Winslow held his finger to his lips and pointed to the badge on his chest. The woman nodded that she understood, then, with a hopeful look on her face, she signed, "Do you read sign?"

"Yes, I do," Winslow signed back. His father-in-law William, Longbear had taught Winslow's nephew, Adahy, ALS although both could hear perfectly. The boy had taught Winslow.

"Oh, good," she signed. "I felt the walls shake. A bit later, I saw something fly into the backyard. I went into the hall and her door was open, but she should be at work.

"I'm a widow and I live alone. I was scared, so I called it in." Her hands moved so fast; Winslow could barely read them.

"Do you think someone is still in there?" Winslow signed.

"I don't know," the woman signed, shaking her head.

"Please, go inside your apartment and lock the door," Winslow signed.

When Winslow heard the door close below him, he lifted his gun, pushed the door open and stepped quickly into the apartment. In the living/dining area, debris was spread across the floor. Broken plates, glasses, torn books, and bric-a-brac. He could see it in the open kitchen, which was also empty. He edged toward the open bathroom door, from which a steady drip, drip, drip could be heard. Light coming in from a window that had to be on the far side of the bathroom cast a rectangle of light on the rug. The square of light was shadowless. Anyone in the room had to be out of the way of the window.

With his finger on the trigger, Winslow peeked around the bathroom's doorframe. The shower curtain was open. No one was in the room.

If someone was hiding in the apartment, the only place left for them to be would be in the bedroom. There were no sounds now but for a lawnmower running somewhere outside. Moving carefully, over to the wide-open bedroom door, Winslow got down on the floor and peered around the edge of the doorframe.

As the bottom of the bed faced him, there was nowhere to

hide behind the bed. The bed itself was too low to hide under. The only spot remaining where an intruder could hide was the double-doored closet abutting the kitchen. The doors were open about an inch, as if they hadn't been shut properly.

Winslow stood. At the same time, his cell phone rang. Ignoring the ringing phone, he stepped into the room and moved quickly to the right and placed his back against the right-hand wall. He half expected anyone hiding in the closet to bolt, but he'd have an advantage, as he'd already have a drop on them before they could get a drop on him. His cell phone stopped ringing.

"You in the closet, come out with your hands up," Winslow demanded loudly.

His demand was met with silence. It was so silent, in fact, he began to believe the intruder had already left, but that was no reason to discard caution. As a sniper in the military, he had lain quiet for days at a time.

The problem was the folding doors of the closet opened from the middle out. He scanned the room. There was nothing in sight he could use.

Getting down on the floor again, he inched over to the door.

When the center of the doors were only an arm's length away, Winslow reached out with his left arm. He grabbed the edge of the door and pulled it open. A squirrel ran out and disappeared around the corner of the closet.

Scanning the floor under the hanging clothes, Winslow saw that no one was there.

As he stood, the squirrel chirped at him from the windowsill.

Winslow went to the window and examined it. It had been broken from the inside. A glance down at the backyard below, revealed a broken frame on the ground by the trunk of the tree that abutted the window.

Winslow's soft knock on the older woman's door on the

first floor got no answer. He shook his head, remembering, and pushed the bell button. The door was opened so quickly, Winslow guessed she had been hanging out near it. A red-and-green light just inside the door was flashing—a deaf person's version of a doorbell.

"The apartment above is empty. Whoever broke in is gone now," Winslow reassured the woman.

"Oh, good. I was so scared," she signed.

"You don't need to be scared."

"Can I get your name and phone number, Ma'am?"

With sign, she spelled out J-U-N-E B-R-O-C-K-H-A-R-T. When he had written down her name, she signed, "What if whoever broke in comes back?"

Thinking it was just a burglary, Winslow signed, "It's very unlikely a burglar will come back. Whoever it was probably already took anything of value. Do you know the name of the person who lives there?"

The woman nodded, then spelled it out L-O-R-I. I'm not sure of the spelling of the last name. Something like M-E-I-S-A-K."

"Thank you," Winslow said. He handed Mrs. Brockhart his card. "If you see or feel anything else suspicious, contact the sheriff's department. Stay in your apartment and lock your door."

She had called in the break-in, so she obviously had access to a hearing-impaired phone.

June seemed to hesitate. Then she signed, "Do I know you?"

"I don't think so," Winslow signed.

"Were you in the newspaper?"

"Yes."

"You saved that kidnapped girl?"

Winslow couldn't help but smile. The notoriety he'd received over a lost hunter embarrassed him.

"That was a brave thing to do," June signed. "It is a pleasure to meet you."

"And you," Winslow signed. "Remember, anything suspicious, contact the sheriff."

In the backyard, Winslow found what was left of the frame lying face-down on the grass. A thin sheet of glossy paper lay half in and half out of the frame. Avoiding the broken glass, Winslow turned the frame over.

It read:

.

Lori Mysek

is hereby awarded a

Career Diploma

for completion of the program of

Private Investigator

.

"Well Lori, if you're a P.I., it looks like you pissed someone off," Winslow said to himself.

CHAPTER 8: VICTOR

June 28, 2022: 2:22 p.m.

As soon as he heard the door close below him, Victor knew it was time to make his way back to the car. As he drove off, his heart was beating wildly.

Instead of getting on the highway, he drove west on the frontage road. He turned off onto the first side road heading north. There were no trees by the road, it was open fields. The road soon turned to dirt and wound up through grassy hills. Once he was out of sight of the frontage road, he pulled over. No one was around. Some deer grazed off to his left near an old, dilapidated cabin whose roof was caving in.

He thought for a moment about the PI diploma. When he'd first been arrested for starting the fire, before he'd pleaded guilty, he'd told Lori he was innocent. When the police refused to look at any other suspects, she wanted to hire a private eye to help investigate, but the costs were so steep they could never afford one. So, Lori started looking into the case herself. She had just signed up for an online course to learn how to conduct an investigation, when Victor decided to plead guilty for a reduced sentence.

"You can't plead guilty," she'd cried. "You didn't do it.

He remembered her face when he said, "The thing is, I did start the fire. I wanted to put it out and be a hero. I did it for you."

He had been surprised by her anger.

Now, as he opened Lori's address book, some pressed flowers fell out. His wife had also decorated the opening page of her address book with drawings of flowers. There was a 'this book belongs to' beneath her drawing. His name and Lori's name were written there, but his name had been crossed out. He felt like he was being stabbed in the heart.

He turned to the B listings and found his name. Here, his name had not been crossed out in the listing. Little hearts decorated both sides of his name. Hope filled his chest. She still had feelings for him, he told himself.

He turned the page. Another set of hearts appeared on that page. The name 'Jeffery Boothe' also had hearts around it. His address, 587 Bearmouth Street, was just a few blocks away from her apartment.

Just to be sure Lori hadn't put hearts by other names, Victor went through every page in the address book. His and Jeffery's were the only names with hearts.

Victor found Jeffery's apartment quickly. He was on the first floor and, as with Lori's apartment, the outer door to the vestibule was not locked when Victor tried it.

Victor double-checked the mailboxes. 'Jeffery Boothe' was handwritten in crisp block letters on a label pasted to the mailbox marked 1A.

Victor went to the man's door and knocked. The knock echoed in the lobby. There was no sound from behind the door.

Victor knocked again. Again, there was no sound.

Victor tried the doorknob. To his surprise, the door wasn't locked. He eased it open.

"Hello," he called, "Anyone home?"

There was no answer. With a quick look around the hallway, Victor pushed the door open wide enough to slip inside.

With a click, the door shut behind him. It was a small studio apartment. A queen-sized bed sat in one corner, covered in a purple comforter. Next to it sat a night table. A dark-stained chest of drawers sat between the open door of what Victor assumed was a bathroom by the light coming through it, and what he guessed was most likely a closet.

Framed on the wall near the door was a diploma—a master's degree in Social Work from the University of Montana. Next to it was a picture of a man at a podium. The caption read Jeffery Boothe is awarded social worker of the year.

Victor felt his blood begin to rise as he looked back at the bed. The pulse of a building headache throbbed at his temples. Victor imagined his Lori in that bed, getting pregnant in this bed. He imagined his hands around the guy's throat. He imagined squeezing the life out of the man who had made him a cuckold.

Using his left hand to lift the mattress, Victor felt between the mattress and the box spring. What he expected to find were sex toys. Instead, he found a cheap .38 caliber revolver. He slipped the gun into his pocket.

He was right about the door on the other side of the chest of drawers being a closet. Suits, shirts, and pants hung on hangers. There was a plastic bag from a dry-cleaner's that rustled when he pushed it aside. In the back corner of the closet, he found a baseball glove and an aluminum baseball bat. He picked the bat up and weighed it in his hands. He took it with him.

In the kitchen, he opened the small white refrigerator. Two cans of Pabst Blue Ribbon beer sat on the top shelf next to a carton of milk and a Tupperware container. Putting the baseball bat under his right arm, Victor took a beer in each hand.

It was growing dark outside. Victor had been sitting in the one easy chair for hours when he heard a sound at the door. He was up, and in the bathroom, out of sight, before the door opened. He'd decided to wait in the apartment, rather than in his Explorer—in case the man came home, and Lori was with him. If Lori was with him, they'd never let Victor in.

Victor heard the man sigh and the sound of the door of the refrigerator opening.

Victor stepped out of the bathroom and moved quietly

toward the kitchen with the baseball bat held firmly in both hands. The man's back was to him. He was smaller than average sized with slumped shoulders. The skin around the back of his head at the hairline looked pink, as if he had just gotten his golden-red hair trimmed.

"Where is my beer," the man said in surprise as he explored his refrigerator.

"I drank them," Victor said.

"What?" The man turned. His green eyes were wide as he took Victor in. His pale freckled skin grew white.

"You Jeffery Boothe?" Victor demanded.

The man hesitated for a moment, then said, "Yes. Who the hell are you, and what are you doing in my apartment? Get out, before I call the police."

Victor calmly walked up to Jeffery and, thrusting the baseball bat like a pool cue, hit Jeffery hard in his solar plexus.

Jeffery made an oomphing sound and doubled over.

"I asked you a question," Victor said.

When Jeffery, who couldn't seem to breathe, didn't answer, Victor swung the bat at Jeffery's knee. It connected with a loud cracking sound.

Jeffery made an airless scream and toppled over.

"Are you Jeffery Boothe?" Victor asked.

Jeffery, huffing air, managed a weak, "Yes."

"You the Jeffery Boothe who got my wife Lori Mysek pregnant?"

If Jeffery looked fearful before, now his eyes widened with new terror.

"No," Jeffery said. "She told me she was pregnant, but it was not me. It couldn't be me. I had a vasectomy."

"I told her I never wanted to have kids."

"But you bedded her. You fucked my wife?"

Jeffery, holding his broken knee, tears streaming down his face, looked at a loss for what to say. He nodded.

"Were you like her caseworker?" Victor asked, glancing toward the diploma and framed photo on the wall.

"Yes, I tried to help her," Jeffery pleaded.

"By knocking her up? What would your bosses think of that?"

.

When Victor got ready to leave a half hour later, he was convinced the guy had no idea where Lori was, and that the man obviously had no real feelings for Lori. Victor threw the somewhat bloody baseball bat at Jeffery's television. The screen cracked, and the set hit the floor with a crash.

Victor smiled to himself, thinking that after the beating he'd just given him, the guy probably wasn't going to be able to get into anyone else's wife's pants for a long time, if ever. But the thing was he was back to square one. The only other lead he had was the logo on the man's truck.

He walked back to Jeffery, who was curled on the floor in a fetal position. Jeffery whimpered as Victor stepped close. Patting the man's pockets resulted in a smartphone and a wallet.

The Wallet had $63 in it. Victor pocketed the cash.

He found Lori's number in a list of speed dials. He considered calling but decided against it. He didn't want her to know he was coming.

A lifer in prison who sold contraband smartphones had once shown him how to look up things on the internet. The prisoners used it mostly for porn. Victor hadn't enough money to buy a phone, but now he used what the guy had taught him to look up the Hamilton Hurricane Motel. There was a map to the side of the listing page. The motel wasn't all that far from where Lori had forced them off the road.

Jeffery, who was lying on his back with his left leg twisted under him, moaned.

"Hey," Victor said. "If I get you some aspirins, do you mind if I spend the night? I don't really have anywhere to go."

Jeffery just looked at him with the one eye that wasn't

swollen shut.

"I'll take that as a yes," Victor said. He went to the bathroom. There weren't any good drugs in the medicine cabinet. He did find a bottle of aspirin.

He put two aspirins on the floor near Jeffery's mouth.

"Gonna have to eat them dry," Victor said. "I think I'll take a shower."

When he was done with his shower, Victor realized he hadn't searched the waist-high oak cabinet that sat in the corner of the living room.

"You don't mind, do you," he said in Jeffery's direction. The guy looked so still; Victor wondered if he'd died.

Pulling open the door, revealed six bottles of liquor. There was an unopened bottle of Jamison 18, a bottle of Drambuie, with a half empty bottle of Johnny Walker's Black Label. Next to the Scotch, was a bottle of Irish Mist and a bottle of Gordon's gin. A clear liquid in a bottle with its name in Cyrillic letters, Victor assumed was vodka.

Victor grabbed the Johnny Walkers and the Drambuie. He found ice in the little fridge's icebox, as well as a brown, unlabeled box. He put the box on the kitchen counter and filled a rock glass he found with ice.

He filled the glass halfway with Johnny Walkers, then added Drambuie to top it off.

As the taste of the Rusty Nail hit his lips, he sighed with pleasure.

People hid all sorts of things in freezers. But he was a bit surprised when he pried open the box. The large baggie of marijuana and a package of cigarette papers looked too good to waste.

CHAPTER 9: LORI

June 29, 2022: 6:21 a.m.

A crow, cawing, woke Lori from a dream. At least she thought it was the crow, who continued cawing a few more times.

It had been an enjoyable dream while she slept, but now the dream bothered her. In it, Jeffery Boothe had come to her door bearing a bouquet of flowers. He told her he loved her, got down on his knees and asked her to marry him. She woke before she could answer him.

She had seemed so happy in her dream that Jeffery was asking to marry her. But if he actually asked her now, would she want to marry him?

Just weeks earlier, they had been naked in his bed. They had gone to his house because he had to go to work early in the morning, and she lived close by, so it would be no problem for her to walk home after breakfast. She had basically seduced him. It had been a very long time since she'd had intercourse with someone she loved and who loved her.

"Come on, I want you," she'd teased him.

"I have to tell you something," Jeffery said.

"I think I need to wear a condom. I had a vasectomy two months ago. But I need to be tested to make sure my semen is sperm free."

"Don't you want to have children?" Lori asked in surprise. She had been dating Jeffery for 3 months.

He had told her more than once that evening that he loved her--something he'd been saying since their third date. She could tell by the way he looked into her eyes that he meant it.

Jeffery didn't answer at first. He sat up and began searching the drawer of the night table at the side of the bed.

"I hope I don't change my mind and want a son someday," Jeffery had said, "But I don't think this is a world I want to bring children into."

Lori felt her heart flicker. She had always dreamed of having at least one child. But right then she wanted, no needed him to make love to her.

If he had the vasectomy months ago, wasn't that all they needed to be safe?

If by some chance she got pregnant, then wouldn't that mean it was meant to be?

She didn't know until her gynecologist explained to her that it can take up to three months for a man with a vasectomy to be completely free of little swimmers.

She remembered his eyes just days ago, when she said, "I have a little surprise."

"What?" Jeffery had asked.

"I guess your vasectomy didn't quite take yet. I'm pregnant."

Rather than the loving look she had expected, hoped for, Jeffery's face became dark.

"I told you I don't want children," Jeffery said softly.

"Maybe God wants you to have some?"

"No! Don't you understand? I don't want to bring children into this shitty world!"

Lori said nothing.

"You need to get an abortion."

The reasonable tone he was taking was making her angry.

"No," she said. She shook her head.

"You have to get an abortion!"

Lori suddenly felt smaller than she had ever felt.

"No. I will not get an abortion. I believe abortions are

justifiable for ethical reasons. But there is no ethical reason here," she'd said.

As she headed for the door of his apartment, he said, "I cannot support you in any way."

At home, after she'd finished crying, she fell asleep.

.

When she awoke in the morning, the sun was hitting the mountain tops across from the sliding glass doors of her motel room.

She woke with a question weighing on her mind: Would she ever find someone who could love her and whom she could love? Now that she was having Jeffery's baby, would that even be possible?

She realized she never wanted to see Jeffery again.

Outside the window, the sun seemed to bring the morning to life.

She had slept in her underwear, which she shed now as she got ready for a shower.

.

The shower refreshed her. When she had dried herself, not having any other clothes, she put her waitress uniform back on.

Going to the front door, she peeked outside. There were about three cars in the lot. They were parked in front of different rooms. A moment later Issy came out of the room next door, pushing a cart laden with linen, some spray bottles, and a laundry basket.

The woman was whistling and looked happy to be alive.

"Well, good morning," Issy said.

"Morning," Lori replied quietly, a little embarrassed about all the personal business she had shared with the woman the night before.

"Do you need a ride somewhere?" Issy asked. "To get your car, or whatever?

"I don't drive," Lori said. "I walk to work and once a week,

Betty, a co-worker and I go to Missoula in her car to grocery shop.

"A ride to work, then?" Issy asked.

Lori shook her head. "I don't think that's safe. Victor is sure to look for me there."

"So, nowhere to go?"

Lori nodded.

Issy studied her. Then smiled. "We had a full house last night. I could be using some help with the rooms."

Lori looked at her.

"I can tell Shay I said you can pay for your stay by helping me. What do you say?"

"You sure it will be alright with Shay? He wants me to be out of sight if Victor shows up."

"You can always hear cars coming up the road. Plenty time to hide. And it's up to me to hire someone. You want to be that someone?"

"Thank you," Lori said, brightening. What do you want me to do first?"

"Well," Issy said, studying her. "We have a pretty good collection of women's clothes in our lost and found. Why don't we find you something else to wear, first? Otherwise, someone might come in and order breakfast."

Issy took her to a room off the office where the lost and found boxes were. There were nine of them.

"I need to take the oldest box to Good Will soon. The stuff in there is about three years old."

"Does Shay live here?" Lori asked.

"Yes," Issy said. "His apartment is on the other side of the office.

Lori was silent. The idea that Shay might come out anytime soon made her heart beat faster.

"Somethin wrong girl?"

"I'm afraid of Shay finding me out here. He was really adamant about my staying in the room. Are you sure it will be okay with him, my being out of my room? Much less working with you?"

"You don't need be afraid Shay throw you out. He not be that kind of man. He could be a blue-eyed devil with the ladies, but instead, he be a good, kind man. I will convince him we can hide you fast."

"I just don't know," Lori said.

"You have someplace else to go, girl?"

Lori shook her head.

"It be alright if you work and stay. It be alright, too, with Issy if you just stay in your room. It be up to you."

"I'll feel better if I'm working," Lori said.

Issy smiled. "Now let's find you some clothes, we got rooms to clean."

It didn't take Lori long to find some sweatpants that fit, a white T-shirt, a maroon U of M Grizzly sweatshirt and a pull-on black cloth hat that completely hid her hair.

CHAPTER 10: VICTOR

June 29, 2022: 8:27 a.m.

A voice, an almost pleading voice, brought Victor Bleché back to consciousness with a head-numbing hangover.

"Hello, yes, my name in Jeffery Boothe," the voice was saying.

Victor closed his eyes. His mouth felt like a dried prune.

"Yes, and my address is 17 Bearmouth Street, Drummond."

In his alcohol muddled mind, Victor thought maybe the person was ordering food. Forcing his eyes open, Victor eyed the two bottles near him. There was a tiny bit of scotch left. He picked up the bottle and chugged the liquor down. It almost made him gag, but he kept it down.

Good old hair of the dog.

"I've been attacked in my home," the strange sounding voice was saying.

Victor tried to figure out who was speaking. There was a silence which didn't help. Victor looked around. Where was he?

"I don't know," the voice said. There was another silence. "He broke my knee and my arm. I think some ribs are broken. I can't see out of my left eye. I can't walk," the voice became almost hysterical. "I can't get out of here by myself."

Suddenly, Victor remembered where he was. He staggered as he tried to get up off the guy-who-made-him-a-cuckold's bed and stand up. The bloody baseball bat leaned against the night table.

Fighting to keep his balance, he moved as quickly as he could into the living room. Jeffery Boothe was on his stomach, cradling a cell phone in his left hand. Victor could see what looked like a bone protruding from the man's right forearm.

"Yes, I know who it is who attacked me," Cuckold-Maker was saying. "His name is..."

The bat made a loud smacking sound as it smashed the cell phone into Jeffery Boothe's head. Blood spattered, some of it on Victor's pants' leg.

Victor bent down and looked at the one eye of Jeffery's he could see. To Victor, he looked pretty damn dead.

He knew 911 wouldn't let it go. Maybe they even heard the smack the bat made. The cops would be here soon.

He had to think quick. But, first things first. He had to wipe everything down. He found a towel by the sink and started wiping the fridge. But as he wiped the handle and door down with it, he realized he'd never remember all the things he touched.

There was only one thing he could do. Taking off the iron grills and stacking them in the sink, he removed the stove top and blew the pilot lights out. Then he turned all the burners on full.

As the smell of gas filled the kitchen, he found a box of matches in one of the kitchen drawers.

In the living room he headed for a Christmas candle he'd seen earlier.

As he lit it, he thought he heard Jeffery groan. Victor picked up the bat and walked over to the man who still lay prone on the floor. Victor thought he could hear the man breathing. He lifted the bat and was about to hit him again when he thought, no. Let the asshole burn. Taking the bat with him, he walked out the apartment door.

CHAPTER 11: SHAY

June 29, 2022: 7 a.m.

Jeremy Brett saying, "Come Watson, the game is a foot," woke Shay from a dream at 7 a.m. The Sherlock Holmes alarm had been a gift from his mother, Julie, when Shay was 17.

Julie had died a year ago.

As Shay came to consciousness, he shook off the dream he had been having as he woke. He was with his ex, Annelle, in their bedroom in Florida. He had been trying to grab her, and she jumped out of bed, naked and giggling. He had watched her walk to the bathroom and was thinking how beautiful she was. But as he turned toward him to say something, it was no longer Annelle but Lori.

His dream bothered him. Lori was attractive, but she wasn't anyone he would want to be in any kind of relationship with.

Getting dressed quickly, he went into the office to see if there were any reservations on the computer from online reservation services. The services took some of his profit, but they were good for letting travelers know the Hurricane even existed.

As he walked to the main desk computer, he saw a woman, out the window dressed in casual clothing, her head covered with a black-knit hat, pushing the motel's spare cleaning cart along the walkway.

Had Issy found someone?

Lori had just walked into an empty room as he came out of the office. He walked to the door and looked inside.

He watched Lori plug in a vacuum cleaner and only when she turned, did he recognize her. "What are you doing?"

"She be working for us," Issy said behind him. "I need help and she is here. So, I put her to work."

Shay turned and stared at Issy. "But she needs to be out of sight!"

"No reason she can't hide real quick. And we be hearing cars coming.

Shay didn't answer right away. "Is she any good at cleaning rooms?" Shay asked.

Issy smiled. "She be very good, boss. Almost better than me."

Lori's was looking at her in disbelief. Shay almost laughed at Lori's expression. Shay trusted Issy with most things, but she had at times a tendency to exaggerate. He just hoped she wasn't exaggerating about their ability to get Lori hidden if needed.

For now, though, they did need the extra help.

After Issy and Lori went back to work, Shay thought again of the limping man who had looked so angry as he chased the young woman around his Explorer. He felt sure now the man had seen the motel logo on the side of his truck. The question wasn't if he would come, but when he would come looking for her.

As Shay walked back into the office, a white Toyota Corolla pulled into the parking spot in front of it. A bumper sticker identified it as a rental from Great Falls.

Shay stopped at the office door and held it open while a worried looking woman in her 40s, with shoulder-length brown hair, got out of the driver's side. The woman smiled at him before she opened the rear driver's side door and helped a small girl with blonde curls out of a child's seat in back.

The woman's face looked pained, but she forced another smile as she passed Shay. Shay closed the door once they were inside.

The woman, taking in the empty front desk, turned to

Shay. "Are you?"

"At your service," Shay said.

"Do you have a room?"

"Yes, we do. Just the two of you?"

"Yes. Unfortunately,"

Shay could tell there was feeling behind those words.

The little girl whose hand she was holding began to fidget.

"Chrissy, stop that!" the mother said. She had to let the girl's hand go while she filled out the registration. The little girl quietly walked around, apparently taken in by the flowers in the office.

He was getting Adrienne Murphy, the name on her Wisconsin driver's license, her key card when she asked. "Are you a private detective?"

Shay looked up to find her staring at his Private Investigation Certificate on the wall above the desk.

He was about to answer, no.

Adrienne was looking into his eyes. Her blue eyes burned into his with an intensity.

And then, Chrissy vomited.

"Chrissy?"

"Is she all right?" Shay asked, eyeing the yellow goo on the floor.

"I hope so. I am so sorry. She gets car sick," Adrienne said.

"Not a problem," Shay said, with feeling. This woman was obviously having problems. "There are paper towels in the restroom over there if you'd like to clean Chrissy off. I'll take care of the rest."

As he stepped out of the office door, Lori came out of room #1 with the cleaning cart.

"Lori," Shay called. "Can you come quick and bring the cart?"

.

As Lori began to wipe up the child's vomit with a paper

towel, Shay handed Adrienne her key card.

"Thank you. I'm so sorry."

"Not a problem," Shay assured her.

Adrienne was about to step away when she remembered her question.

She opened her purse and took out a sheet of paper.

"Have you heard of Timber Marsh's Treasure?"

Shay thought a moment. "Yes, I've seen something about it on the news. And I think we've had a few customers who mentioned they were looking for it."

"Okay," Adrienne said. "Well, I need a private detective to help find my daughter who went looking for it and who I have not heard from in days. She always calls every night when she is away, but for the past three days there have been no calls."

Shay was about to say that he was not a licensed PI and that there were a few in Missoula who could help her when she continued.

"Well, there is a poem that Marsh published in his book about how he hid the treasure. May I read it to you?"

Shay nodded.

The woman went out the door and was back in a minute with a book. She opened it to a page marked with an envelope and read:

.

"From the wag-made abode of fishing creels
You must launch your outlook high
But do crawl beneath the wheels
And worm your way to sunlight's eye.
The portal points neath the lines that sing.
To rocks and logs that form a ring
Round the path the deluge did forge.
The way will lead to a narrow gorge.
Up the slopes where sagebrush rests
Up to where you see the sky

Pass by the beargrass's soft white breasts
For that is the way my treasures lie
Look for the tower--a cannular snag
A malingering finger on a faceless hag.
That is the way that you must follow
To the heights of a shadowed hollow
For there you'll find what you seek
Hidden in the mountain peak."

•

"That sounds like Quake Lake," Lori said, standing. "The starting point, that is."

"You know where it is?" Adrienne almost cried. "Are you sure? I've had no idea as to where to start looking."

"It sounds like it. Wag could mean an earthquake, and it is a popular fishing spot. I spent some vacations there with my family when I was a kid. I did a lot of exploring. There is an area by the boat launch area that fits that description to a T."

"But all these people on the internet say they have the right solution," Adrienne said, the desperation back in her voice. "Most think it's by a bend in a river. And the search area can be anywhere from New Mexico to Montana."

"Well, I met Timber Marsh when I was a kid. This was before he hid the treasure. He and his wife rented a cabin near my family's." Lori said.

"That doesn't mean Mrs. Murphy's daughter was searching there," Shay pointed out. "You could be right about the treasure, but not where Mrs. Murphy's daughter...."

"Harper," Adrienne said.

"Harper was looking," Shay finished.

"Harper told me she was going to Yellow Bone," Chrissy suddenly said.

"She told you she was going to Yellow Stone?" Adrienne asked her daughter, bending down to look at her.

"She said she was going to stay in the beaver's creek," the

girl said. "And if she found the treasure, she was going to look at the geezers."

"Beaver's creek campground?" Lori asked.

Chrissy nodded in affirmation.

Hope seemed to radiate from Adrienne.

"Look," Adrienne said, turning to Shay. I researched private investigators in Montana. I have $1500 I can give you in cash right now as a retainer if you can go look for my daughter." And I'd be able to pay you $100 an hour if it takes more than that.

"I have the degree," Shay began to explain, "but I am not a licensed Private Eye."

"I passed the same investigation course," Lori said. "And this qualifies as a wilderness search and rescue and not a private eye issue. If he won't look I will."

"How are you going to get there?" Shay asked, suddenly feeling as if something was being taken away from him, even though he'd just refused it.

"It would be safer if we go together," Lori said. She looked at Adrienne. "I take it time is of the essence?"

"Yes, she could be hurt," Adrienne began to cry.

"As long as you understand that we are not private investigators and are acting as a rescue team," Shay found himself saying.

"I will write that down if you want," a now hopeful Adrienne Murphy said. She bent down, picked up Chrissy and held her in her arms. "They are going to find Harper," she said to the child.

The little girl smiled.

"And we will need the retainer," Lori said.

Shay gave her a look.

"We will need supplies. I need hiking shoes, for example. Canteens, a first aid kit."

"I have a canteen and a first aid kit, but the first aid kit is the motel's, so I suppose I should leave that here."

"Here," Adrienne said. She held out a stack of $100 bills and quickly counted off 15.

Lori took the money and handed it to Shay. "I'll take Adrienne to her room. And get all her information about Harper. While you get what supplies you have on hand?"

Shay nodded. He wasn't sure how he felt. He was about to do his very first investigation. And with a woman he rescued from a possible murderer as a partner?

He watched Lori lead Adrienne, who was again holding Chrissy's hand, out the door.

CHAPTER 12: LORI

June 29, 2022: 10:29 a.m.

Lori returned to the office with a photo of Harper Murphy, a description of Harper's car, her license plate number, and an idea of what the young woman's tent looked like. Plus, she'd gathered some miscellaneous facts, like the girl loved Mountain Dew and Hersey's Chocolate bars.

In the motel lobby Lori found a tent, two backpacks, a single canteen, and other equipment in the middle of the floor.

"I have this older backpack," Shay said holding up a somewhat dusty green canvas backpack with an aluminum frame, "that you can use.

"As you can see I have a new one with a water bottle built in that I can access with this little hose. So the canteen is for you."

Lori browsed through the pile. There was a pair of binoculars, a headlight, a stack of energy bars, matches, a candle, toilet paper, and a ton of other things that could prove useful.

"I filled the canteen for you and the water container in my backpack," Shay said. He handed Lori a walkie talkie with a plastic lanyard. "I've set these to channel 18. That way we can communicate if we get separated."

Lori nodded as she took the unit. It squawked as she turned it on. "New batteries."

"No," Shay said. He turned his on and pressed the side button. "Testing."

His voice came out of Lori's unit. "We better get some extra batteries for it," he said over the speaker.

"Can you think of anything else we might need?" Shay asked after they both turned their walkie-talkie off.

"I'll help you get this stuff packed. I do need hiking boots, and we might need a first aid kit," Lori said.

"We can get that in Deer Lodge. And maybe think of anything else on the way," Shay replied.

Lori had been a little uncomfortable as she got into the passenger's seat of Shay's truck. She dreaded the conversation she thought that might ensue. But the first thing Shay said was, "I have a compass," but maybe we should get a GPS unit." He looked at her. "Or two, one for each of us."

Lori pulled a notebook and pen from her purse. "Let me write this stuff down. And we'll need batteries for those, too.

"GPSs will be expensive though, wouldn't they?" Lori asked.

"There's a pawn shop," Shay said. Maybe we'll get lucky."

•

The tall thin man at the pawn shop set two older GPS units on the counter. "They both work," he said. "This one is $30 and this one is $60."

"Why is the black on more?" Lori asked.

"A better model," the man said. "And I do try electronics out when I get them. They both work."

"We'll take them," Shay said. "And this pair of binoculars," he added, pointing to a pair in the glass case the GPS units rested on.

"We should both have binoculars." he said to Lori.

"And one of those?" Lori asked, pointing at some headlights hanging from the wall.

"Yes," Shay said. "We both need to have one."

•

As they entered a nearby department store, a thin young man who had to be just out of high school with curly reddish brown hair and freckles stepped up to them.

"Can I help you find anything?" he asked enthusiastically. A matronly clerk at a cash register gave the boy, whose name-tag read RANDLE, a smile.

"I don't think so," Shay said.

"Maybe," Lori said. She ignored the look Shay gave her.

"We are looking for," she hesitated, "a friend who seems to be missing on a hike. We need a first aid kit and any other equipment you carry that you think we might need?"

Randle thought for a moment, "I'm on it."

"Wait," Lori said as Randle began to walk off. "I have a list of what we already have. We won't need anything already on the list."

Randle took the open notebook.

"I hope you can read it," Lori said.

Randle looked down at the book. He squinted. Then he smiled, "I think so. Let me go look."

Randle started to turn and then stopped. "Where is this person lost?"

"We think West Yellowstone. Near Quake Lake," Shay said.

Randle nodded and moved off.

Shay looked at Lori with what looked to her like admiration. "You made a list of our supplies? Including what we just got at the pawn shop?"

"It's just a habit with me," Lori said.

"That was good thinking."

"Thank you," Lori said. A warmth washed over her. And suddenly, she felt a little more confident. It was the first time he'd complimented her.

Lori found hiking boots and a wide-brimmed cloth hat.

Shay, who had not thought to bring a hat, picked out a Missoula Osprey baseball cap.

Although the team had changed its name, he liked the old Osprey name better.

As they headed back to the counter, Randle came up with a shopping cart seemingly filled to the brim. He handed Lori back her notebook.

"My Dad is a Search and Rescue volunteer, and I've helped him pack," Randle said.

He looked up at Shay, who was staring wide-eyed at the cart.

"If there is anything you don't want, I can put it in another cart and put it back,"

"Wow," Shay said, taking in the stuff.

"Or, if you don't use it, you can bring it back for a refund."

"Then maybe we should take it all," Shay said.

Shay pushed the cart to the checkout counter.

As Shay put the items on the cart in front of the smiling cashier, Lori wrote them down in her notebook: duct tape, sun block, hand warmer packets, scissors...

"What's this?" Shay asked as he took out an aluminum object that looked like a number 8, with a smaller circle in the middle. Protrusions like horns on the largest circle made it look a bit like a bull.

"It's a rescue 8," Lori said. "It's for rappelling. I did some in high school."

"The area you mentioned has got numerous cliffs," Randle said. "So, I added three harnesses, two 100 foot climbing ropes, some carabiners, pitons, and a small hammer for securing the pitons in case you need to do any climbing in your rescue."

"And we can return it if we don't use it?" Lori asked.

"Yes," the woman at the cash register said.

"I don't know anything about the kind of climbing you need those things for," Shay said.

"I do. And Harper could be somewhere where we will need it."

Shay thought for a moment and then put the rescue 8 on the counter.

.

It was almost 200 miles from Deer Lodge to the Beaver Creek Campground in West Yellowstone. For most of the drive, they were silent. Lori felt a little like there was an elephant in the truck they were ignoring. Victor. She tried to concentrate on the rolling green countryside. There was hardly any traffic coming toward them and no cars in sight going in their direction.

When they saw a sign for Ennis, Lori said, "We can get gas there, and something to eat."

"I really didn't think we'd be spending that much," Shay said. The bills at the pawn shop and department store had taken $431.33 of the money Adrienne had paid them.

"I have a little cash," Lori said. "I can pay for lunch. If you're worried about money."

"And if there is no sign of Harper, I think we should give Adrienne her money back." Shay said.

"I agree," Lori said.

Lori didn't know how to read him. But she'd just learned he was the kind of guy who'd give a desperate woman her money back. She found herself admiring him a little.

"You are right," Lori said after a bit. "But we should keep a record of the gas we use. It is fair that we get our expenses back.

"And," Lori said. "If we do find Harper. Or even a sign of her being in the area, and even if we have to call in Search and Rescue to help, then I think you've earned the money."

Shay looked at her. "I've earned it?"

"You keep the money and let me keep my room for, say, two weeks."

"Okay," Shay said. He was quiet for a while, then said, "But I will pay you for housekeeping then. It's only fair."

"It's a deal," Lori said.

CHAPTER 13: WINSLOW DOYLE

June 29, 2022: 3:57 p.m.

Winslow Doyle towered over Erlinda Dugaduga, the 5' 2" ME with the bowl-cut, dark hair in the cold sterile room. All the hair beneath her ears had been shaved, and it gave the young doctor an almost puppet-like look. "This body is that of a male, as indicated by the pelvic bones." Erlinda said into a microphone attached to a headset. "This male body number 547520 was recovered from a fire caused by a gas explosion in Drummond. The body shows the deep charring, indicating the fire burned with quite intensive heat."

It wasn't Doyle's first body. But it was his first burn victim. Charred pointed bone fragments protruded from the blackened corpse, partly curled in a fetal position.

There was a click as Erlinda turned off her recorder.

"So, when, big tall and handsome, are you going to ask me out on a date?" Erlinda asked.

"I am happily engaged, as you know," Doyle said.

"You are too good-looking to let yourself be tied down. You are not married yet," Erlinda teased. Looking into his eyes, she added, "You have time to trade up."

Doyle smiled, although with the body in front of him it wasn't easy. At least it didn't smell. He felt a little queasy as it was, and if there had been a smell, he didn't know if he would have been able to keep from vomiting. "I am afraid you are out of my league.

"But what can you tell me about this body? Did the fire curl him up this way? Did it break his bones."

"You are right about the Dugaduga being out of your league." She took a breath then continued. "The fire did curl him up and heat can break bones, but the fire did not break these bones. This man was beaten repeatedly with a heavy blunt object before the fire."

"So, he was beaten to death?"

"No," Erlinda said. "The inside of his lungs are seared. He was alive when the gas explosion occurred. And, as you probably figured out, this was a murder."

.

Jeffery Boothe worked in the social services' office, just a short walk away from the state lab. Jeffery's supervisor, who Winslow had called from the ME's lab, was crying as he walked into her small office.

Debby Bethworth was a slightly plump woman who tinted her brown hair with a purple dye. Her hair matched the color of the large framed glasses she wore.

As Winslow stepped into her office, she lifted her glasses with her left hand, and rubbed her right eye with her right hand, leaving a mascara smear.

"I'm sorry to have to question you about this, but time is of the essence," Winslow asked. "What can you tell me about Jeffery Boothe?"

"I've worked with him for 11 years. I can't believe he's dead."

Winslow looked at the woman. She was visibly shaking. He'd try to get through this as quickly as possible. He'd just take it one step at a time.

"Did he have a girlfriend?"

Debby looked up and seemed to hesitate.

"This is no time for keeping confidences." Winslow said sternly. "The man is dead. He was murdered. Any information you have might help me catch his murderer."

THE MISSING TREASURE HUNTER

"He had a girlfriend. Her name is Lori Mysek. Jeffery was very upset in the last few days. I asked him why. He just said something unexpected had occurred and he had to break up with Lori.

"Was Lori Mysek someone who could be violent?"

Debby shook her head. "No, I don't think so. She seemed sweet. The kind of person who wouldn't hurt a fly."

"So, do you have any idea what the problem was about?"

Debby wiped a tear from her eye. "I think they were getting serious. But Jeffery had a firm belief that it wasn't right to bring children into this world.

"To that end, he'd had a vasectomy a few months back. I suspect the young woman wanted to have children. And had a problem with that."

Winslow left with a list of all the accounts that Jeffery Boothe serviced for the department of social services. But the first person he wanted to talk to was Lori Mysek.

The fact that her apartment had just been broken into might just be a coincidence. But Winslow didn't believe in coincidences.

CHAPTER 14: SHAY

June 29, 2022: 3 p.m.

"I think we just passed the road to the fishing access," Lori said.

Shay looked into the rearview mirror. "I didn't see a sign."

"I don't think there is one. But Beaver Creek Campground is just up here?"

The sign for the campground appeared, and Shay slowed and turned onto the paved road that wound up through a thick forest of Aspen and pine trees.

At the top of the hill they found a large camper/trailer on the left-hand side of the road set up with a picnic table, and barbecue grill. A hand-painted sign on a wooden board read SIGN IN HERE. A board handing from a piece of twine read: Be Back Soon.

At the end of the board was a little brochure holder. Shay stopped the truck. "Can you get us one of those?"

"Sure," Lori said.

She came back with a folded map of the campground. "Looks like there are three sections. Which way do you want to try first?"

"Let's go left," Shay said.

They'd decided after leaving Ennis, if they found Harper's tent but not Harper, they pick a campsite as near to Harper's site as possible.

They had hoped to show Harper's photo to the camp host, but as the host was gone, they'd have to wait.

Each wing of the campground swung around a heavily

wooded area. Many of the sites were set up with tents, and many others with campers of varying size.

They knew Harper had a small blue pup tent and kept their eyes peeled for it. But as they neared the end of the last camping loop, there was no sign of a tent resembling Harper's.

Many of the sites had yellow tickets on them. They discovered that these meant the sites were reserved for the night. As they came up to the last campsite in the last loop, a little alcove among the trees, Lori said, "Stop."

Shay eased to a stop and looked at the site. "You're thinking we'd better grab it before they're all gone?"

"We should probably put our tent up to claim it," Lori said.

Shay pulled the truck into the site.

Grabbing a fee envelope from a stand by the nearest outhouse, Shay filled it out while Lori unrolled the quick-setup tent.

"I think we should go back to the boat launch," Lori said as she began to get the tent into shape. "I think if Harper was reading the clues the way I'd read them, that is where she'd start."

CHAPTER 15: LORI

June 29, 2022: 3:47 p.m.

On the way out, Lori saw a man come around the back of the host's trailer.

"I think the host is back," Lori said.

Shay pulled the truck over. Lori got out with the photo of Harper in hand.

Ross Haines was short, and in his late sixties. He smiled at Lori as she approached him.

"How can I help you?" Ross asked.

"Do you know if this woman checked in?" Lori asked. "She was coming here, but she hasn't been in touch with her mother, and her mother is worried."

Ross took the photo and looked it over carefully. "I didn't check her in. But my wife might have. And she is out doing rounds. Can I keep this? I can ask her when she gets back."

Lori thought then shook her head, no. "It's our only copy. I'll try to catch your wife later. But, thank you."

"No problem," Ross said.

It was a short drive to the turnoff onto the boat ramp access road. As they bounced down the potholed road, Lori scanned the area she remembered from years ago.

Lori was looking back toward the mountain on the other side of the highway, when Shay said, "I think I see her car."

A somewhat dusty, green, slightly battered VW Beetle sat parked next to a truck with a boat trailer on the left-hand side of the road.

"And there's a state trooper here for some reason," he

added.

The Montana State Police cruiser was parked on the other side of the road.

A short female trooper in a Smokey Bear hat was talking to a heavy man with a protruding belly holding a fishing rod. A fishing net and cooler were by the man's feet.

At the sight of the trooper, Shay's stomach felt queasy. Although he desperately needed the money, if he were caught working as an unlicensed private detective, he'd never even get a training license. He decided the best thing to do was ignore the officer and go about their business.

He pulled in next to the VW and said, "Listen!" He was about to warn Lori to stay away from the State Trooper, but Lori was out the door before he turned the engine off.

The VW had been backed into the spot and a license plate was not visible in front. All the windows were rolled down a crack.

Lori quickly walked around back. As Shay got out of the truck, he watched in horror as Lori made a beeline toward the lady trooper.

"We've been out on the lake fishing since about 9 a.m.," the man was saying. The man glanced back at a short woman with frizzy black hair and black rimmed glasses who was sitting on the grass and wiping tears from her eyes.

The trooper was young, and pretty, with dirty blonde hair. She was so petite, the sidearm on her hip looked like it might topple her over.

"Well, I have your information," the trooper was saying as Lori stepped up, "and I'll put out an APB on the truck. We might get lucky."

"Excuse me, officer, is this by any chance about a stolen vehicle?" Lori said as Shay caught up to her. A look of fear crossed his face as he realized he was too late to stop Lori from talking to the trooper.

The trooper looked directly into Lori's eyes. "Do you know

something about the vehicle?"

"My boss and I are looking for a missing hiker. We believe that is her Volkswagen over there. But the plates are missing. If the there is a stolen vehicle, the VW's plates might be on it."

"Do you know her license number?" The trooper, whose name tag read Hasslet, asked.

"It's ABE 172DZ, and that car fits the description we were given of our missing treasure hunter's car. We've never seen the car before.

"So, we were hoping you might look up the plate number for the car that is sitting over there based on the VIN," Shay chimed in. That way, you'll have a better idea if the thief might have also stolen the VW's plates.

"I can do that," Hasslet said, and started walking to the Volkswagen.

Lori tagged along. "Great! It would really help us to know if it is Harper Murphy's vehicle before we spend time searching this area. Her mother is very worried about her. And we don't want to waste time here if we have no evidence she'd been here.

The trooper read the Vin and wrote it down. "Do you know if this person likes soda and candy bars?" Hasslet asked as she looked into the car's window.

"Hersey bars and Mountain Dew?" Lori asked, hopefully.

"Bingo," Hasslet said, walking back to her vehicle. She left the car's door open as she checked the vin.

A few minutes later, the young officer handed Shay a slip of paper with the VIN number. Beneath the VIN, she had written Green VW registered to Harper Lynn Murphy. She turned to the man whose vehicle had been stolen and said, "I've put out an APB for your truck with your plates and with the plates of the VW over there."

The man nodded.

Shay took out his phone and tried calling the motel. Issy could tell Adrienne that they had found the car.

"You won't get a signal here," Hasslet said.

Shay shrugged. "I wanted to let her mom know we found her car."

Hasslet paused for a moment. "How long has this person been missing."

"Her mother said she didn't call Saturday," Lori said.

"She's been looking for Timber Marsh's treasure," Shay said. "And we guessed she might be in this area. Her car confirms it."

"Her car confirms someone parked it here," officer Hasslet said. "If you can find some evidence that she is actually lost up there," Hasslet nodded toward the mountain, "I can get a search and rescue team in."

"That would be great. Can we contact you with a walkie-talkie if our cells don't have a signal?" Lori asked.

"If I'm within range of your signal. But since you found her car, and it is likely she might be in this area, I can drive by more often just in case.

"Use channel 9."

Hasselt thought for a moment. "You better tell me who you are."

Once Lori and Shay had given Hasslet their details, Lori asked, "Any chance you could contact the motel where we work and leave a message for her mom that we found the car?"

Hasslet considered this, then nodded. "Give me the number."

They left officer Hasslet to the couple and retrieved their backpacks from Shay's truck. Lori led them along a path through high grass between the lake and an open field next to the highway. Butterflies flew from the new flowers and other insects buzzed around them.

"It's easier to follow the path than bushwhacked the field," Lori said.

"Where are we going?" Shay asked.

"Well," Lori began. "The fact that her car is here means, if she was the one who parked it here, I was right about her thinking like I do. So, going, by the first lines of the poem:

"From the wag-made abode of fishing creels

You must launch your outlook high.

"This is Quake Lake. A wag can be a shaking movement. Therefore, this lake is the wag-made abode. And I think launch your outlook high means we have to go up from the boat launch. Which means up this mountain in front of us."

Lori pointed to the rising mountainside in front of them, topped with trees and steep spires of rock amid wide washes of grass.

"I explored here as a kid. After my mother left us, my Dad'd come here to fish, and since he was all I had, he brought me with him."

"Your mother left you?" Shay asked.

"When I was nine," Lori said.

"Anyway," I didn't like fishing that much, so he'd let me either stay in the car to read or explore. I explored a lot. I know this area pretty well.

"Okay, so the next line of the poem is:

"But do crawl beneath the wheels

And worm your way to sunlight's eye."

"Have you memorized the poem," Shay asked.

"Pretty much, but I have Adrienne's copy of the book in my backpack just in case."

They had been following a path that cut across the center of the field. They rounded some high brush and an open concrete-fronted tunnel running under the highway appeared.

As they got close, Shay could see the other side was open to the sun.

"I don't think we actually have to crawl, but it will take us beneath the wheels," Lori said, crouching just a bit as she stepped into the ridged-steel pipe that formed the inside of the tunnel.

•

As they stepped back out into the light at the far end, Shay asked, "Okay, what's next?"

"The portal points neath the lines that sing.

To rocks and logs that form a ring"

"There should be electric lines up ahead, and then we'll just have to see."

They made their way through some trees and when they emerged the wires were clearly visible.

"So far so good," Shay said. He pointed at the ground. "Are you seeing the crushed grass. Someone walked this way recently."

"Good eye," Lori said. "Let's see if we can find us rocks and logs that form a ring."

A few moments later she bent down and picked up a fairly straight fallen branch about two and half inches thick and 6 feet long. "Just what I needed, a walking stick."

"Should find one myself." Shay said. He found one a little further on and broke a few branches off.

They soon surmounted a crest. The slope of the mountain above them formed what looked like a mile-wide ski-jump. They stood on the lip of the jump. Above them, a long gully snaked up the mountainside. A washed-down pile of rocks and debris at the base of the gully formed a crude circle.

"It must have been hard getting along without a mother?" Shay suddenly asked.

Lori was quiet for a moment. "Can we just concentrate on trying to find Harper?"

"If that's what you want."

They started walking toward the gully. "What's the next clue," Shay asked.

"Up the path the deluge did forge.

The way will lead to a narrow gorge."

"I guess we go up the gully then" Shay said.

CHAPTER 16:
VICTOR

June 29, 2022: 10:06 a.m.

Victor drove by the Hamilton Hurricane Motel and looked the place over as he did so. The white Adirondack chairs made him think of a place his family used to go to in the Dakotas. He imagined for a moment sitting on one of those with Lori across from him--the two of them enjoying a beer and the weather.

About a city block past the motel, he pulled into a driveway almost hidden by willow and pine trees. At the top of the driveway sat a tree-shaded double-wide trailer. Steps led up to a covered porch in front of the door. Hanging flowers hung from eaves. The driveway led to a turnaround in front of the trailer. Victor drove all the way in and kept an eye on the door as he made the loop.

No one came out to see who had driven in.

The motel was completely out of sight due to the woods. Victor thought about parking right there in the drive and checking out the motel on foot. But decided against it. Whoever lived here might come back and call the cops. Still, if he needed to come back at night and the place was still empty, it was a good place to hide his SUV.

Deciding that the direct approach was best, he drove over to the motel and parked in front of the office.

He was surprised to find a tall, skinny black woman behind the desk. He got right down to business.

"I'm looking for a young woman who, I believe, got a ride

from a man driving a truck with the name of this motel on it," Victor said. He held out a snapshot of Lori.

The woman blinked. "I think boss say somethin about he give a woman a ride. He take her to Butte, I think."

"Why would he take her to Butte?" Victor asked angrily.

The woman looked startled. She raised her forearms out making a big W and shrugged her shoulders. "I no know why boss man do."

To Victor, the woman looked reasonably confused. But he just wasn't sure he trusted her.

"When is this boss of yours coming back?"

The woman shook her head.

Victor thought for a moment. "Give me a room," he demanded.

"We need credit card, number on license plate, and what kind of car."

"I don't have a card. I have cash," Victor said, an edge to his voice.

"Okay," the woman said. "Cash work."

.

The room wasn't bad and the bed soft. Victor realized he was exhausted. But he decided he'd check the place out first.

There wasn't much to the motel, but as he stepped into the laundry room, his eyes opened wide. Lori's waitress uniform was hanging from a clothes hanger on a rack to the side of the machines.

Grabbing the dress, he rushed back to the office.

The tall, skinny woman took a step back as he stormed up to the desk.

"You know who belong that dress?" the woman asked.

"This belongs to the woman I'm looking for. Do you know anything about it?"

"I wash it," Issy said. "It clean now."

Victor stared at her. "Are you stupid? Was this in a room?

Does she have a room here?" His voice was steadily rising.

Issy shook her head, no. "That dress I find in room over here." She led Victor through a door into a room lined with shelves filled with fresh linen. "It be right here by found and lost things." Pointing to a line of boxes on a table, she thought a moment. "Maybe boss let her change to lost clothes?"

Victor wanted to shake the skinny slut. He imagined his hands going around her neck and squeezing.

"Boss will know when he get back," Issy said.

Victor just looked at her for a long time. He had to fight back the urge to hit her. But he couldn't tell if she was lying. And he needed to be able to stay at the motel until the boss did get back.

"Thank you," he said.

CHAPTER 17: WINSLOW DOYLE

June 29, 2022: 6:47 p.m.

"Who is it? Please position your mouth by the peephole, so I can read your lips." June Brockhart asked through the closed door. Her voice had that unnatural tone that people who once had hearing but have lost it many years before seemed to drift into.

To Winslow, the woman still sounded scared. He moved, so his lips were directly in front of the peephole. "Deputy Doyle, Ma'am. I was here earlier."

The apartment door opened a crack and a brown eye stared out at Winslow.

A moment later, the door opened all the way.

"Yes?" the woman signed.

"Do you have any idea if anyone has been in the apartment above since I last saw you?" Winslow signed.

"No, officer," June signed, shaking her head.

"Thank you," Winslow signed. "Please lock your door again."

•

At Lori's apartment door, Winslow knocked softly. The light touch of his knock pushed the door open an inch.

He listened. No sound at all came from inside.

Taking out his revolver, he cleared the interior of the apartment quickly.

He needed a clue as to where Lori Mysek might be. He

decided to start his search in the bathroom. The medicine cabinet contained only a razor, a box of replacement blades for the razor, feminine shaving cream, aspirin, bandaids and mercurochrome. There were no prescription drugs that might need to be refilled. Of course, the woman might have taken her prescription meds with her.

There was a wastebasket under the bathroom sink. Reaching into his back pocket, Winslow removed a pair of nitrile gloves, which he slipped on.

The top layer of the basket was covered in tissues. Poking carefully with a single finger, Winslow probed the tissues.

About half-way down, he touched something hard. Getting his fingertips around it, he lifted it from the wastebasket. It was a home pregnancy test.

Winslow assumed the plus in the little window meant the test had been positive.

A search of the rest of the apartment gave up no clues as to where Lori Mysek had gone.

He was just about to go down and let Mrs. Brockhart know that he was leaving and that she should call him if she detected anyone going up to the apartment above when his phone rang.

"Hi sweetie," Winslow said. He'd been expecting a call from his fiancée, Shawna Edwards. She was taking care of some final details for the ballroom where their upcoming wedding reception would be held.

"Well, hi sweetie to you," the very male voice of Deputy Tom Bedder replied. "Although, I did not know you felt that way about me."

"Hello, Tom," Winslow replied.

"Listen. I did a check on Lori Mysek. No wants or warrants. No police record at all. I just sent her driver's license photo to your cell."

"Okay, thanks," Winslow said.

"But get this," Bedder continued. "The husband is Victor Bleché. And Bleché just got out of prison two days ago.

"The name sounds familiar," Winslow said.

"He set a fire in an airport hangar where he worked because he wanted to be the hero that put it out," Bedder continued, "Did millions-of-dollars-worth of damage."

"So, he's out on parole?"

"Yes, he's on parole. He did most of his time. But they put him on parole to keep track of him. I called the prison about him. The first month of his sentence, he 'accidentally' broke his right calf. A while later, the guy they suspected of accidentally breaking Bleché's leg died in a mysterious fire. They had no proof, so they never charged Bleché with the murder."

CHAPTER 18: SHAY

June 29, 2022: 5:49 p.m.

They had been climbing for almost 45 minutes. The mountainside was steep, and Shay found himself out of breath. At times, they were able to walk in the center of the swath the melting snow and rainwater had cut down the mountain. But at other times piles of debris, mostly bark-stripped logs, large boulders, and dirt set up blockades that smelled of earth, had to be skirted.

Currently, they were skirting one such pile, the size of a pickup truck.

"Let's take a break," Shay said. He tried to sound authoritative, but to himself he sounded like he was pleading.

"Okay," Lori said, coming to a stop. She leaned on her walking stick and put her left hand on her hip.'

"How do you do it?" Shay asked. "You don't even look winded?"

"Getting tired?"

"Yes," Shay admitted, "You don't seem to be too much worse for wear, and you're pregnant."

Lori looked annoyed. "Just because a woman is pregnant doesn't mean she can't be in shape."

"I didn't mean anything," Shay said.

"I run 3 miles a day. And I'm not that pregnant. I found out a few days ago. I was late and bought one of those tests."

Shay knew that late meant she had missed her period. It brought back a bad memory of Annelle. He thought they wanted to get pregnant. They even talked about having a child. But after she had moved out and in with Houlihan, the man he had caught her in bed with, he had found the hidden birth control pills she had been secretly taking.

"Did you want to be pregnant?" Shay asked, realizing the instant the words were out of his mouth that he had no business asking something as personal as that.

"I wanted to be someday," Lori said. "The timing just wasn't planned."

Looking at her, Lori somehow seemed vulnerable at the moment. His heart went out to her.

Embarrassed, Shay looked away down the mountainside toward the earthquake-made lake. Sweeping slopes, green with brush and grass, were dotted with islands of evergreen trees. Here and there, gray-blue rock poked up like faces coming out of the earth. The dark water far below gleamed blue-black, with the trunks of dead trees rising from the depths like stubble on a partly whiskered face.

Shay turned back to Lori and saw she was sitting on a log, with her backpack propped in front of her. There was room on the log next to her, and it looked like the only place around to sit.

"Is that place taken," Shay asked, pointing next to her on the log.

Lori waved her open palm toward the spot next to her. Shay took it as an okay.

As Shay sat down, he took in Lori's skin at her hairline. He could see her hair roots were a darker blonde, but the highlights she added gave her more of a golden look. Some beads of sweat had formed on her neck and the side of her forehead. To Shay, her skin looked flawless.

Lori wasn't as beautiful as Annelle. But she was very pretty.

"What's the next line in the poem?" Shay asked after a time.

Lori looked to her backpack and opened a flap. She slipped the book out.

"Wouldn't it have been easier to copy it to a slip of paper?" Shay asked.

Lori gave him an unreadable look.

"I mean as far as the weight goes?"

"There are photos in the book. I thought we might see something that matches a photo, and there are plenty of photos."

"Good thinking," Shay said.

"I think we need to consider a few more lines this time," Lori said and began to read:

"Up the slopes where sagebrush rests

"Up to where you see the sky

"Pass by the beargrass's soft white breasts

"For that is the way my treasures lie."

"Well," Shay said. "We can see the sky from anywhere. So, I think it means we have to go to a spot where we can see the sky through the trees at the top of this mountain."

Lori turned and looked up above them. "There are more bear grass blooms above us," Lori observed.

Shay had always thought the bear grass flower looked like women's breasts. Each white globe was shaped differently, with a nipple-like tip at the top.

"They're my favorite flower," Shay said.

"Cause they look like boobs?" Lori asked.

Shay just looked at her.

Lori giggled and looked back at the book. "This is what I think we are looking for:

"Look for the tower--a cannular snag

A malingering finger on a faceless hag.

"That is the way that you must follow

"To the heights of a shadowed hollow.

"So, I think," Lori continued, "We're looking for a tube-like finger on a topless tree that's going to point where we need to go,"

Shay nodded. Whatever Lori was, she was certainly smart.

"Are you rested enough," she asked.

Shay was, but he would have said yes even if he wasn't. "Let's race up the hill," Shay said.

Lori laughed. "We'd better save our energy. We don't know what we are going to find up above."

CHAPTER 19: ISSY

June 29, 2022: 4:48 p.m.

From the window, Issy watched the man walk down to his room, open the door, and go inside.

She could feel herself shaking. The man scared her. Her late father, Winston Wint, was a drunken fisherman who beat Issy's mother, Issy, and her brother. Issy could always tell when her father was about to go on one of his rampages.

She had the same sense for this man, even though he did not appear to have been drinking at all. She looked down at his name in the logbook. Victor Bleché. She trembled. She entered the license plate number he'd given her into the computer. If the man was being looked for by the police, it would help them find him.

Picking up the phone, she pushed the speed dial for Shay's cell. Her heart beat wildly in her chest as she listened to the rings on the other end. Finally, Shay's voice mail came on.

"You've reached the phone of Shay Hamilton. Please leave a message."

"This is Issy," Issy said. "Lori's husband just checked into the motel. I would have told him we were full but, honestly, I was afraid to. The man scares me.

"Please get back to me and let me know what you think we should do. I'd call the police, but I don't have any real reason to."

Issy took a deep breath and continued.

"He discovered Lori's waitress uniform in the laundry room. I told him you had given the woman clothes from the lost and found. I don't think he really believed me. I told him you took her to Butte.

"You should have seen his face. I actually felt, he wanted to attack me.

"Oh, crap!

"Adrienne and Chrissy Murphy just stepped out of their unit and I can see Victor walking toward them. I've got to try to do something.

"Call me."

Issy rushed out the office door. She reached Adrienne and Chrissy just as Victor did.

"Mrs. Murphy," Issy said breathlessly. She just knew it was important to speak before Victor did.

"Can you come to the office? Quickly. We've found some information for you."

"You did?" Adrienne asked. "Did they find Harper?"

Victor looked as if he were about to speak. And Issy knew she couldn't allow Victor to show the photo to Adrienne or Chrissy.

"Please hurry," Issy said. Without answering Adrienne's question, Issy turned and rushed back to the office.

Only when she reached the door did she turn back. To her relief, Adrienne was just a few steps behind, tugging Chrissy along with her. Victor stood where they had left him, looking angrily in their direction.

As soon as the door shut behind Adrienne, Issy spoke," Do not tell that man that you saw the young woman who is looking for your daughter. He is her abusive husband and a very dangerous man."

Adrienne looked startled. "So, you haven't heard anything about Harper?"

"Why is he dangerous?" Chrissy asked.

"He is the kind of man that likes to hurt people," Issy said. "There are bad men in this world like that."

She looked out the office window. Victor was still

standing in the same place. Issy knew that during the day it was impossible to see through the office window. But Victor, taking what looked like a defiant stance, seemed to be glaring right in at them. Adrienne followed Issy's eyes. As Issy turned to her, Adrienne started shaking.

Just then, the phone rang. "Look," Issy said. "There is a nice trail through the woods that starts behind the office. I can take you out through the apartment, and you can avoid having to lie to him."

Adrienne nodded.

The phone was still ringing, but Issy ignored it. There was no guarantee Victor wouldn't come into the office. She led Adrienne through Shay's apartment and out the back door.

"Trail's right over there," Issy said, pointing through a gap in the trees.

"Thank you," Adrienne said, as she took Chrissy's hand and led her away.

.

Back in the office, Issy could see Victor pacing back and forth, keeping watch on the office door as he did. She felt her own heart beating faster.

As she went behind the desk, she saw the message light on the phone was red.

Thirty seconds later, Issy was racing up the walking trail, trying to catch up to Adrienne and Chrissy.

CHAPTER 20: SHAY

June 29, 2022: 6:47 p.m.

Lori was walking a little ahead of Shay. They were making their way through a copse of trees when Lori cried out. "There!"

Shay emerged from the trees and saw it. The very tall dead tree had but one lone branch high up. The branch, ending in a gray finger, pointed up the mountain.

Shay's heart was beating fast.

"She might not be too far away, now," Lori said.

"Let's hope," Shay said.

The slope of the mountain grew steadily steeper. Twenty-five minutes later the two of them literally hit a sheer stone wall, directly in front of them, rising far overhead. It stretched out for over 50 yards on either side of them.

"You sure this is where the tree limb was pointing?" Shay asked.

Lori nodded. "I took a compass reading."

Shay thought a moment. "Then it had to be the wrong tree."

"Did you see any other trees?"

There was nothing he could say to that. They both stood silently. It was a chance to catch their respective breaths.

"I don't see anything that could be a cave from here," Shay said, looking upward, "and how could we possibly climb to a cave up this flat wall?"

"We are thinking about this the wrong way," Lori said.

"Huh?"

"We are not looking for the treasure. Harper was. What we

need to ask ourselves is: If Harper came up this way, what would she do if she found this wall?"

"Go around?" Shay suggested.

Lori nodded. "I'll go right, and you go left, if that's okay with you."

Shay looked off to the left. On that side, the grass, and trees rose up as the stone pulled back further. On the right, trees touched the wall itself only 50 yards away. "Okay. Let's keep in touch on our walkie-talkies."

As he walked away, he had a strange feeling. In a déjà vu flash, he felt as if he and Lori had somehow done this before.

CHAPTER 21: LORI

June 29, 2022: 7:18 p.m.

As Lori walked along parallel to the wall, she tried to think of what Harper would do. Obviously, if the young woman thought the treasure was in the mountain, then she'd have to go around it. But the line of trees ahead of her hugging the wall did not look like a viable way to go.

When Lori was within a few feet of what were mostly lodgepoles, she had no choice but to descend. The trees were so close together, that was all Harper would have been able to do.

If the young woman had gone this way, there had to be a trail through the trees.

About 20 yards down, Lori found an opening. The deer trail that snaked into the trees was only a foot wide.

Lori examined the path. A few feet in, what looked like a footprint from a medium-sized boot was clear in a small section of soft dirt.

Lori keyed her walkie-talkie. "Found a footprint in a deer trail that could be hers."

A moment later, Shay replied. "I found a deer trail too. But I haven't seen any footprints. There's an open spot up ahead with a stump someone could sit on. Let me check a little further. If I don't find anything, I'll come back your way."

After walking another 50 yards through the trees, Lori heard the sound of running water. The trail began to curve around the mountain. Lori clicked on her walkie-talkie. "I'm rounding the mountain. Might be some stone between us soon. Don't know how well this thing will carry. Just letting you know."

The radio crackled.

"I'm coming your way. I found some beer cans buried under a log by the stump. Also, some field stripped cigarettes in the dirt. Don't think they are Harper's. That VW did not smell like someone smoked in it. So, I don't think she went this way."

"Roger that," Lori said. "Good catch smelling the VW. I didn't think of that."

"Thanks," Shay called back. "Where did *Roger that* come from?"

"Television," Lori replied.

She began to move faster along the trail. As the sound of water grew louder, the trees seemed to thin out.

Another 50 yards along the trail, the trees opened. Below, in a narrow gorge, water rushed to a roaring waterfall.

The trail, what there was of it, curved, and narrowed to a narrow dirt path that hugged a ledge on the side of the mountain. Lori approached the trail cautiously. The tracks of a medium size shoe were clear here.

She lifted the walkie-talkie and pressed send as she walked along.

"There are more tracks here. They go around the side of the mountain," she heard her own excitement in her voice.

As she walked further, the ledge became even narrower. At the point where the ledge was only a foot wide, the tracks seemed to end.

Lori's heart began to beat wildly. She hoped what she saw didn't mean what she knew it would mean. There were no tracks leading back.

Suddenly, a bird flew out from some hole in the rock wall along the ledge in front of her. Lori gasped, jumped back without thinking. For a moment, she thought she might lose her balance. She grabbed at the wall, catching a slightly protruding rock, with which she was able to catch her balance. Her heart raced. It took her a moment to stop shaking.

Finally, calming herself, Lori peered over the lip of the ledge. The cliff face, here, plunged hundreds of feet down. But about 25 feet below on a six-foot-wide balcony that seemed to be covered with grass and debris lay a body, face down. A purple zippered sweatshirt opened on either side of her torso like wings. The sweatshirt's hood had fallen over the person's head, so their hair was not visible. There was a black-looking circle in the debris, Lori took to be blood seeping away from the hood. Harper?

Lori had to fight the rising bile in her stomach to keep it from erupting.

She grabbed her walkie-talkie and keyed the talk button.

"I'm right behind you," Shay said from right behind her.

Startled, Lori turned quickly. As she did so, her left foot slid in the soft dirt. Her right arm went out and hit the stone wall. Suddenly, she was pitching toward the chasm.

She felt a strong hand grip her arm, and just as suddenly she was being pulled away from the edge.

"Sorry," Shay said. "I didn't mean to startle you."

Lori could barely breathe. She looked at him. "I'm just glad you have quick hands."

"So she went this way?" Shay asked.

"She only got this far," Lori said, pointing below.

Shay peered over the ledge, then let out a long whistle.

"I need to get down to her," Lori said.

Shay looked over the side and shook his head. "How?"

"I can rappel down. I can at least check to see if she'd still alive."

"She doesn't look like she's breathing."

"It's too far to see from here," Lori said. If she's been there since Sunday, she'll need water…"

"Maybe I should go down," Shay said. In response to Lori's hard look, he added. "I'm stronger than you."

"No!" Lori said, shaking her head. "You're stronger than

me. You're much more likely able to bring me back up than I'd be able to lift you."

"Right."

Once the rope, rescue 8, pitons, carabiners, small hammer, and two of the harnesses had been assembled on the ledge, Lori found three cracks. Into each she hammered a piton, a sort-of wide triangular nail with a loop at the top, to act as anchors. After locking a D-shaped carabiner to each of the loops on the now secured pitons, she ran the climbing rope through the carabiners to the midway point. Then she tied large knots into the two free ends of the rope.

"You've done this before?" Shay asked, admiring how quickly Lori set up the equipment.

She paused in adjusting the harness and said, "Yeah, my senior year in high school. I dated a guy who liked to climb. "The only thing I actually did was this, rappelling. It was fun."

Before stepping off the ledge, Lori held both sides of the rope and gave the rope a tug. All three pitons making up the anchor seemed secure. Before she thought about it too much, still facing the rock wall, she leaned back and stepped over the ledge so that she was literally parallel to the mountain and walking down.

It took her less than a minute to reach the ledge where the figure was lying.

She stood for a moment and looked back up.

Shay's head peeked over the ledge. His look of concern was obvious as he peered down at her.

Lori picked her way through the debris on the lower ledge toward the prone figure.

"I'm not sure what I need to do to make sure I don't hurt her worse than she already is," she called up to Shay.

"Just go with your instincts. I'm gonna see if I can contact Hasslet."

As she stepped close to the prone figure, she thought she saw the back of the sweatshirt rise. Bending down, she placed her hand on the back of the sweatshirt. She felt a heartbeat at the same time the figure groaned.

"She's alive," Lori called out. Somehow, she knew it was Harper.

Gently, she pulled the hood back. Reddish blonde hair covered part of the young woman's face. Lori lifted the hair.

The face was partly covered in dried blood, but it was recognizable.

"It's Harper," Lori called out.

"I've got Hasslet on the radio. How badly hurt is she?" Shay called back.

Lori freed the canteen she'd attached to her harness. Lori opened the canteen and sprinkled some water on the young woman's face.

Suddenly, Harper moved. The young woman tried to press herself up with her hands. She groaned and cried out in pain. Twisting, she turned herself sideways.

"Whoa!" Lori cried, putting her hands gently on the young woman's shoulder, "Don't attempt to move just yet. You have to be careful. Does anything feel broken?"

"My left leg might be. I can't feel it now," Harper said in a weak voice. And my left wrist hurts like hell. That's why I screamed when I tried to get up. "Do you have any water?"

Lori offered her the canteen. Harper grabbed it and began chugging water down. Lori grabbed the canteen and pulled it away. "It isn't a good idea to drink too much too fast."

Harper nodded. "I'm so thirsty. I don't even know how long I've been here?"

"Probably, at least a day, Lori said. "Do you mind if I check your legs? I need to see if anything is actually broken."

"No."

Lori felt along both of Harper's legs.

"I don't think your legs have any breaks, let me check the rest of you?"

Harper endured the probing of her hips but winced when Lori touched her ribs.

"I think you either cracked or broke your ribs," Lori said.

"At least they are not sticking out," Harper replied.

"You do seem to have a nasty bump on your head, but the bleeding seems to have stopped."

"I want to try to get up," Harper said.

"Okay. But let me help you," Lori said.

Surprisingly, Lori was able to help Harper stand.

"Can she walk?" Shay called down.

"I think so," Harper said. "Throw the extra harness down?"

Harper was quiet as Lori began to adjust the harness on her.

Then, suddenly, she gave Lori a suspicious look, "How did you find me? Were you just hiking here?"

"Your mother hired us to find you," Lori said.

"We are not treasure hunters," Shay called down.

"I suppose I should be glad even if you were," Harper laughed, then cringed as the laugh shook her ribs.

Harper's eyes were blackened, and she looked awful, but she seemed with it enough to try to get her off the ledge.

"Lori, I can pull you up," Shay called down. "Then we can lower the rope. All Harper will have to do is attach it to her harness, and the two of us can pull Harper up."

"Just a second," Lori said. She walked to the lakeside edge of the wider ledge she and Harper were on.

"Lower my backpack and then get the rope free. I think it will be easier if we lower Harper from here. There's a spot just a few yards below, I think we can walk down from."

"Okay. I think we'd better get our headlights out," Shay said.

When the three stepped out from the trees on the last stretch of the trail, they saw the lights of an ambulance parked in front of Officer Hasslet's patrol car on the other side of Highway 287.

As Shay and Lori guided Harper across the highway, Adrienne and Chrissy stepped out from behind the ambulance. Hasslet had to hold Adrienne and Chrissy back from running onto the road.

Harper screamed when her mother hugged her.

CHAPTER 22: SHAY

June 29, 2022: 10:35 p.m.

"How are you doing?" Shay asked as they drove up to their tent site. No one stirred in the campground but for one woman holding a lantern heading in the direction of the latrine. Several sights they passed had glowing fires.

"Exhausted," Lori said.

"You don't want to drive back to the motel?"

"I am aching all over, I just want to lie down."

"Do you want me to make a fire and heat something up?" Shay asked.

They had a few cans of chili, some roast beef hash and two beef burgundy freeze-dried dinners they'd brought with them.

"Do you have the energy for that?" Lori asked. "I don't."

"No," Shay said, surprising himself.

"I hear the Campfire restaurant at the fishing camp is pretty good. I think I can wait until breakfast."

"Sound good," Shay said.

Lori's face was dirty, her hair mussed, but she had a smile on her face.

Lori unzipped the tent door and they climbed inside. She turned the lantern they'd brought on, bathing the inside of the tent with light.

"You did an outstanding job up there. I'm impressed," Shay said.

"We needed both of us to get her out of there," Lori said.

"Yeah, but you're the one who rappelled down to her. Frankly, I don't know if I could have done that. That was pretty brave."

Lori was silent.

Shay began unrolling his sleeping bag. When he looked at Lori again, he saw tears making channels down her dusty cheeks.

"Are you okay?" Shay asked.

Lori didn't say anything for a few moments, but then shook her head, no. "I'm not brave at all."

"What you did today took guts," Shay insisted.

Lori looked up at him, her eyes wet in the lantern light.

"That's nice of you to say, but I'm terrified, most of the time."

Shay shook his head. "Why?"

"My husband. The one I'm trying to divorce. He scares me."

"Why did you marry him, then?"

Lori looked away for a few moments, then turned back to Shay. "He was a nice, really dumb, but nice guy when I met him. Super good-looking like a movie star. And quite the..."

She shook her head as if shaking off the thought. "But in some ways, he was very insecure and needy. So, one day he decides to impress me. He was a volunteer firefighter. He set a fire in a hanger where he worked, thinking he could be the hero and put it out. But the fire got going too fast. Planes were burned down to their frames. The hanger was destroyed. And they quickly figured out it was him.

"So, he confesses to get a lower sentence and goes to prison. But he was a 'good-looking guy.' And apparently 'good-looking guys' are in danger in prison.

"When I went to visit him the first month he was there, he seemed frightened. The visitor's room was like an open lunchroom. Whenever another prisoner got close to him, he'd back away. That first day, this one guy touched his arm in passing, and Victor practically jumped out of his skin.

"The last time I visited the Victor I knew, the Victor I married, he told me he had a problem, with this one guy, Anson

Smith. According to Victor, Smith was one of the toughest, guys in the prison, and he wanted Victor to 'be his bitch'.

"Victor had been refusing the man's advances and trying his best to avoid the man.

"The next time I went to the prison, the man had broken Victor's right leg with a barbell. In the hospital ward, Victor cried most of the time I was there.

"I visited him more often while he was in the hospital.

"But the first time I visited, once he was back in the population, he was a different man. He kept asking me to bring things, like girlie magazines. I was embarrassed and didn't want to do this because they searched me before I was allowed into the prison. When I told him 'no' he exploded and cursed me. He even tried to get me to smuggle him drugs.

"I would go visit him on Thursdays on my day off. But then I missed a Thursday. I think I just needed a break from this man he'd become. When I went back the following Thursday, he was livid. He squeezed my arm so hard it hurt me. A guard had to tell him to let go.

"When the guard walked away Victor whispered in my ear, 'I got the man who broke my leg alone in the laundry. I dosed him with gas and burned him alive.'

"I believed him. I hadn't noticed until that moment, but the other prisoners in the visiting room, who'd he'd seemed afraid of before, now seemed to go out of their way to stay away from him.

"I made to leave, and he said, 'If you miss another visit, you'll be sorry.'

"I talked to a lawyer and had divorce papers drawn up. The day I had them delivered to him I got a collect call from the prison. I accepted it.

"'You there?' he asked.

"'Are you going to sign the papers?' I asked back.

'I love you. I don't want to lose you,' he was pleading.

"'You've already lost me,'" I told him. There was no way I'd ever go back.

"There was a long silence on the line.

"'If you ever try to leave me, you'll get worse than the guy who broke my leg ,' he said.

"And then he hung up.

"I didn't visit him again for a year but had to try to get him to sign the papers to finalize the divorce. I received word he'd sign them if I came in. So, I went back again.

"He really wanted to just talk. He kept saying things like he missed me.

"He apologized for threatening me. But I could see in his eyes the threat was still there.

"We left it that he would look over the papers and sign them. But when I went back the next week, he hadn't signed them. He said he had a problem and wanted changes…

"I had my lawyer make the changes. But then he found new problems. This went on for months…

"All I wanted was a divorce. And I told him he could put in anything he wanted. I just wanted out," Lori said, wiping new tears from her eyes.

"So. Finally, I tried to handle it only through my lawyer. I did not go back to the prison. I tried to get on with my life."

Lori stopped. Looked at Shay, who had sat down on his sleeping bag. "I'm probably just boring you."

"No," Shay said. "But when you found someone else, it turned out he wasn't a much nicer guy?"

"He's a social worker, and he is one of the nicest men I ever met. There's a picture on his desk at work. He's holding a little girl whose mother was being arrested. The look in the girl's eyes as she clings to him says it all.

"He is someone you can trust when you need him."

"But don't you need him as you are pregnant with his baby?"

"He told me in advance he would never bring children into

this awful world.

"But I needed to feel loved. And he had had a vasectomy. I thought we were safe until I realized my period was two weeks late.

"I bought a home test kit. It came out positive and when I told Jeff he blew up.

"He wanted me to get an abortion. That is something I just couldn't do. So, he said he never wanted to see me again."

Shay reached out and took her hand.

From the look on Lori's face, he realized she was now feeling embarrassed. And in that moment his heart went out to her.

"My ex changed too" Shay began. After what Lori shared, he felt he should tell her something of his own experience. "We were both 20 when we met. She worked in a coffee shop I went to every morning. And one day she just asked me out. We talked all night on that first date, and I went to the coffee shop the next afternoon and asked her out again.

I think back then she really loved me.

"For example, when I was in grade school--second grade--we decorated tissue boxes as mailboxes for Valentine's Day. Well, I'd been sick with pneumonia for a month. The teacher told my Mom about it just before I went back to school. On Valentine's Day, I hardly got any Valentines.

"So, you know how when you're getting to know someone you like, you share stories. I told her about my first Valentine's Day heartbreak. So, on our first Valentine's Day together, what do I find, but a box like the one my Mom had made for me back in grade school. And in it were about 40 little cards, signed with names like Daffy Duck, Bugs Bunny. I can't even remember all the names. But I felt so loved as I opened them up."

Shay stopped speaking. He found it hard to swallow. He hadn't realized how talking about Annelle would make him feel. Suddenly, he could barely breathe.

"So, what happened?" Lori prompted after some time had

gone by.

"We were both in grad school at the time, I was majoring in theatre, and she was in business. But, still, we got married. And then one day I got home from school early and found her in bed with another guy."

"Wow!" Lori said. She squeezed his hand now. There was sympathy in her eyes.

"I don't understand why she did that," Shay said. "I thought she loved me. I still loved her."

CHAPTER 23: LORI

June 30, 2022: 12:01 a.m.

Lori didn't say anything right away. Somehow, she had this image of Shay as this tough guy. He had certainly seemed cool and somewhat aloof when she stepped into his truck. But now that he'd opened up to her, he seemed more human.

"Did you cheat on her?" Lori asked.

"No. I loved her. I never even thought about it."

Lori thought for a moment. "I've read the common reason someone cheats in a marriage is that they are insecure," Lori said.

"Insecure?" Shay said, "I don't understand why she'd be insecure. I told her I loved her every day."

Lori sensed he was closing up. That he was suddenly embarrassed about sharing his wife's infidelity.

"You were both graduate students. Did you have a lot of work to do for your theatre courses?"

"Yeah," Shay said. "I often had to stay late for workshops or rehearsals We put on two plays a month."

"Did she wait up for you?"

Shay thought. "At first. But I'd be so tired when I got home, we didn't talk much. After a while, she'd just be sleeping when I got home."

"And I imagine there were some attractive women in the theatre program?"

Shay gave her a guilty look. "There were some tempting ones who made it clear they liked me. But I never cheated on Annelle."

"You don't have to be physically apart to feel lonely," Lori said. "When Victor was injured in prison, I visited him as often as I could. But I began to feel lonely when I was with him. He would lie on the hospital bed, his leg elevated in a cast, and barely look at me. "Can I have some water?" was the most intimate thing he asked me.

"You know, I think I'd like to try to sleep now. I'm feeling really tired," Shay said.

June 30. 2022: 7:14 a.m.

Lori awoke to birds singing. She'd pushed her sleeping bag away from her head, and the cold morning air entering the bag made her shiver.

She glanced over at the sleeping form of Shay. Curled up on his side, she could see his back rise and fall.

"Why did I have to tell him my dirty little secrets?" Lori thought. She felt her face flush thinking about what she shared about her relationships with Victor and Jeffery.

And now they both, unfortunately, knew a little about each other's secrets. When she got in moods like this, she had a system to get herself back on firmer ground. She'd ask herself what is it exactly that made her feel this way.

And after a bit she decided it was the way Shay shut their conversation down. It was the way he suddenly did not want to talk anymore, as if he regretted what he had shared with her.

She'd have to decide if she could really keep working at the motel if it was going to be embarrassing to both of them.

CHAPTER 24: ISSY

June 30, 2022: 7:01 a.m.

Issy carried the office wastebasket over to the large steel bin at the corner of the motel parking lot. She could have emptied it later, but she liked getting out in the morning. The air was crisp. A variety of birds sang or chirped a morning melody.

This was her peaceful time before she had to begin cleaning rooms.

As she crossed the motel parking lot, her eyes fell on Victor Bleché's Ford Explorer. Customers didn't always get their license plate number right, but that was not usually a problem. As she glanced at Victor's license plate, she realized she'd entered the number wrong.

She remembered entering the middle part of the plate as the number 360. Now, looking at the plate, she could see that was incorrect. The middle characters read 36O. Instead of a '0' the last of those three digits was the letter 'O.'

Back in the office, she entered the correct license number into the computer.

Twenty minutes later, her phone rang.

"The Hurricane Motel," Issy said cheerfully. "Your peaceful getaway in western Montana."

"Garnet County Deputy Sheriff Winslow Doyle, Ma'am. You just entered a vehicle license plate ABE 36O NYC1925. Is this correct?"

"Yes,' Issy said. "I entered the O as a zero last night. He put a slash through it."

"Is the vehicle still there?"

"Yes, it is in the parking lot."

"May I ask who drove the vehicle there?"

"His name is Victor Bleché. And I have to admit I am a little afraid of him."

"Is he alone?"

"Yes, but he's looking..."

"Ma'am," the Deputy said, interrupting. "Don't say anything to him about this call. I will be there in about 20 minutes."

"Should I try to delay him if he tries to leave?"

"No, Ma'am," Do not interact with the man in any way other than you would for normal motel business."

Issy was stunned to silence.

"Do you understand, Ma'am?" Deputy Doyle's voice boomed out.

"Yes, yes sir," Issy said.

As she waited for the Deputy, she occupied herself with paperwork at the main desk. She couldn't help but glance up every minute or so to check the parking lot.

Ten minutes after the officer's phone call, she saw Victor Bleché walking across the parking lot. Her heart began to leap. Would he come to the office? She was relieved when he walked to his car, got in the car, and drove out of the parking lot.

Five minutes later, a tall, handsome Deputy got out of a Jeep that pulled up in front of the office.

"This be it," Issy said, opening the door to Victor's room. "He pay cash. Did not say if he be back."

"But he said he wanted to wait for the owner?"

"Yes."

"And the owner hasn't been back?"

"No, and I imagine the man's wife still be with Shay. I call them, leave texts. I don't get through. I just hope they not come back."

"You said they went to look for a lost girl?"

"She be found by them last night. On a mountain in West Yellowstone. It be near Quake Lake. State police let her mother know ambulance be taking her to the hospital."

Winslow handed Issy his card. "If Lori Mysek does come back, have her call me. If you do hear from your boss, and she is with him, tell them not to come here or go to her apartment."

The way he said it prompted Issy to ask, "There be something wrong at her apartment?"

"It's been broken into, and this man may be checking on it."

The Deputy began looking around the room. He picked up the room's trash basket and looked inside, it was almost empty.

He went into the bathroom. This trash can was full of tissues. And he was about to reach inside, when Issy said, "No!"

She held up her right middle finger, showing a scar that ran from the quick of her nail to the middle knuckle. "Got this digging in wastebasket like that. What do this, me, just be a razor. They can be needles. People throw all kinds of nasty things away.

"You can empty it out on the floor. I can sweep it up when I do my rounds.

Winslow shook the contents of the basket onto the floor. Most of the basket was filled with tissues.

Issy watched Winslow push the balled up tissues around and then pick up a crumpled piece of paper that had been hidden in the Kleenex.

The deputy spread the paper open, read what was on it, and put it in his pocket.

"That be a clue?" Issy asked.

"I can't discuss it," Winslow said. "Look, this man is dangerous. Do not confront him. Stay away."

"What kind of thing he do?"

"We believe he killed Ms. Mysek's boyfriend."

CHAPTER 25: SHAY

June 30, 2022: 7:21 a.m.

Shay woke when he heard Lori unzipping her sleeping bag next to him. He was still tired. Thinking about his discussion with Lori the night before he knew he wouldn't get back to sleep. He sat up.

Hey," he said. "Good morning."

"Good morning," she replied, glancing at him. She quickly twisted out of her sleeping bag, bent down, picked it up, and began stuffing it into its bag.

To Shay, her greeting sounded somewhat subdued.

"I want to thank you for talking to me last night," Shay said. "I thought about what you said. I guess I thought that Annelle, my ex, slept with that guy because she hated me or something. It didn't occur to me that it was because of attention I neglected to give her. That she was lonely and feeling unloved."

"Was she gorgeous?" Lori asked.

"Pretty much."

"I used to think in high school the prettiest girls had it made. They had all the attention of all the boys. I was jealous."

Shay looked at her. "You are not exactly homely."

"Well, gee, thanks," Lori said, a bit miffed. "I thought of myself as cute. But I'm talking about the stunningly beautiful girls. The top cheerleaders. The ones I and every other girl envied.

"And then one day I was walking home, and I found this girl, Johanna, who was maybe the most beautiful girl in the school, crying by some bushes near the baseball field.

"She was broken up because her boyfriend dumped her. As we talked, I realized how insecure she was. Her entire self-worth depended on how others saw her."

"So, did you and Johanna become friends?" Shay asked.

"No," Lori laughed. "The next day she was with her cheerleader friends in the hall and I said hi. She ignored me."

As Lori was way ahead of him getting her stuff packed, Shay concentrated on getting up and packing his sleeping bag.

When he was done, Lori grabbed the frying pan he'd brought and held it up. "Do you still want to eat at the Campfire? Or we could cook up some of the food we brought with us?"

"Let's eat at the Campfire," Shay said. "We deserve to celebrate."

They were just finishing up loading the truck when a familiar state patrol car pulled up. Mud stained the vehicle's bumpers, and fingers of mud streaked the passenger side window. The shiny vehicle smelled of oil.

"Officer Hasslet," Lori said, as the Zoe Hasslet exited the car.

"I'm glad I caught you," Hasslet said.

"Is Harper alright?" Shay asked with concern.

"Oh, the girl I hear is fine and recovering nicely."

Both Lori and Shay looked at the woman expectantly.

"A deputy sheriff from your county contacted me. Do you know a Victor Bleché?"

"My ex, well, husband," Lori said.

Zoe gave Shay a questioning look, and then said, "Apparently he stayed at your motel last night, Mr. Hamilton. It is believed he was looking for his wife." Zoe looked at Lori.

"Is he still there?" Lori asked. Shay could hear the anxiety in her voice.

"No. A local deputy sheriff went to the motel when Mr. Bleché's license plate was re-entered into the motel computer this morning. He had written down the wrong number when he checked in. By the time the deputy got there, Mr. Bleché was gone."

"Why were they looking for him?" Shay asked.

Hasslet hesitated. "Apparently he is a person of interest in a murder that occurred the day before."

"Who was murdered?" Lori asked.

This time, Hasslet was quiet for some time before replying. "Do either of you know a Jeffery Boothe?"

Shay saw Lori's face crumble. Lori put her hands over her eyes and cried, "Oh, my God!"

"Ms. Mysek?" Zoe Hasslet asked, "I take it you know him."

.

As officer Hasslet drove away, Shay could see that Lori was still shaking.

"What do you want to do?" Shay asked.

Lori looked at him with tears running down her face.

"It's my fault he's dead." Lori cried.

"Even if your ex, I mean husband, killed this guy, it isn't your fault."

"Victor killed him. I just know it. I could see something like this coming years ago if I tried to leave him after he killed that man in the prison."

"So, what do you want to do?"

"Okay, so he did notice the name of your motel on your truck when you drove away," Lori said.

"And that's why he went there. He couldn't find you, and he wants to ask me about where you went."

"Let's go back," Lori said.

"Are you sure?" Shay asked. He had to admit he wasn't that surprised.

"We might as well," Lori said. "He's bound to come looking for you again to find out where you left me.

"He's going to be after me, no matter where I go. And I don't have anywhere else to go. Now the local cops are looking for him. Maybe we can help them find him."

CHAPTER 26: LORI

June 30, 2022: 8:44 a.m.

"I'm not really hungry," Lori said when they pulled into the parking lot of the Campfire Lodge's restaurant. It was the first thing she said since they left the campground.

Since she learned of Jeffery's apparent murder, all she could think of were Jeffery's eyes when they made love that one time.

Shay drove on.

.

At the Kentucky Fried Chicken in Red Hall, where Shay asked if she'd minded if he stopped as he was starving, she hadn't touched her chicken and finished only half of an A&W root beer float.

All she could think about was Jeffery. How he made her laugh. How he'd been so tender with her when they finally made love. How she'd imagined what a life with him would be like. The idea of Victor killing the man clawed at her guts.

She realized she wasn't scared. Victor had been at the motel. He would be coming back to talk to Shay. There was a chance that he would see her. But she didn't care. Just as long as Victor was caught.

Looking down at the table next to her untouched chicken dinner, she noticed the receipt. The date was on the top of the receipt.

"I have an idea," she said as they left the restaurant. There was a trash can in the parking lot. Taking the lid off, she began to rummage inside.

Shay watched her with a puzzled look on his face. A camp robber alighted nearby as if waiting for her to retrieve some treat. She examined the first receipt she pulled out. "Today's." She said as she crumpled it up and put it on the side of the container.

"What are you doing?" Shay asked.

"You'll see. I just hope they didn't have to empty this trash can since Tuesday."

Lori dug deeper. She pulled up another receipt and cried, "Dated Tuesday. Just what we need.

"Put this in your wallet or pocket. If Victor asks you where you dropped me, show him this. Tell him you bought me a chicken dinner and left me here filling out an application."

Shay studied her. "He will most likely head right here then, and we can call the deputy."

"Right."

Shay thought a moment. "We just have to hope nothing goes wrong."

As they turned off I-90 onto the road to the motel, Lori asked, "Maybe slow down?"

"Why?" Shay said.

She could tell by his tone he was anxious to get back to his home.

"I have this feeling..." she said.

The motel was coming up on the left now, and Shay began to slow.

"That's his Explorer," Lori cried. She ducked down below the dash. "What are we going to do?"

Shay was quiet for a moment. "Just relax."

Although she couldn't see, she could tell as he sped up, he was driving past the motel. A few seconds later, she could feel the car turn. Shay pulled to a stop moments later.

"You can get up now," Shay said. "I think you're safe for the moment."

Lori sat up. She was in the yard of someone's home. A beautiful display of flowers hung from the porch of a double-wide trailer.

"I own this. My uncle lived here and had a manager who lived in the apartment behind the office. Issy lives here now, and I live in the office."

"It looks really nice," Lori said.

"All Issy's doing. She painted the place, hung the flowers. Made it her home."

Shay got out. Lori opened the door and stepped out, carefully looking around, expecting to see Victor appear.

"I keep a key with me. I'll let you in and then go over and tell Victor I bought you a meal in Red Hall."

"You should call Deputy Doyle and tell him Victor is here right now," Lori said.

"Right," Shay said, taking out his cell phone. "Issy might have already called, but no need to take chances."

CHAPTER 27: VICTOR

June 30, 2022: 2:06 p.m.

Victor had just paid for another night at the motel in cash when the familiar truck with the motel's name on it passed by on the road in front of the motel. The driver appeared to be alone in the cab.

Suddenly, his head began to throb. He turned back to the skinny woman behind the desk.

"Are you sure you don't know when your boss is getting back." There was an edge to his voice that made the woman behind the counter flinch.

"As I say, I do not know. Can he call your room when he arrive?"

"Yeah," Victor growled. "Have him do that."

Victor stormed outside and looked down the road in the direction the truck had gone. 'Just wait till you actually get here,' he said to himself.

Victor carried the single bag of food supplies he'd bought in Missoula from his Explorer to his room and looked in the mirror over a desk where a brochure about a tour of the old Deer Lodge prison sat.

He looked as tired as he felt. Stubble on his chin gave him a seedy look. He knew a beard might help disguise him if he let it grow out, but shaving was a habit he found hard to break.

Squirting a dollop of shaving cream into his hand, he was just lifting it to his face when the phone rang.

"Crap," Victor said, flicking the shaving cream into the sink. He wiped his hand with a clean towel on a rack by the sink and went to the phone."

"Mr. Bleché, this is Shay Hamilton, the owner of the motel. I understand you've been trying to reach me."

"Yeah." Victor said, adding to himself, 'you smart ass bastard.'

"Well, I'm in the office. I'll be here for a while, and I'm at your disposal."

"I'll be right there," Victor said.

CHAPTER 28: SHAY

June 30, 2022: 2:45 p.m.

Issy seemed to be in shock about Jeffery Boothe's murder, even though she didn't know him.

"If we can keep him here long enough for the sheriff's men and highway patrol to come, it will all be over," Shay said.

There was an unnatural silence in the office. Shay could hear the ticking of the clock.

Issy nodded.

"Would you rather leave?" Shay asked. "You don't need to be here while I talk to him."

"You might be needing backup, boss," Issy said, "That man be coming now."

Out the front window, the man Shay recognized from the Ford Explorer limped toward the office. His leg braced glinted in the sunlight.

Issy moved over to a pile of mail and busied herself.

Shay had never been into any kind of mysticism. He'd heard of things like aura's and knew some people claimed to be able to see them, but he had never experienced anything like that before.

But when Victor Bleché walked into the motel office, Shay felt something cold and dangerous.

The man was smiling as he came in. In his short-sleeved white t-shirt, his biceps bulged. His teeth were crooked and yellowed.

"Well, we finally meet," Bleché said, holding out his hand.

As Shay gripped the hand, the man shifted his grip so that

111

his palm held Shay's fingers and the man bore down hard.

Forcing himself not to wince, Shay said, "We finally meet. Now, how do you think I can help you?"

Shay often thought that the years he spent studying acting had been a waste. It had been Annelle who encouraged him. And his abandoning his dreams of being an actor went with Annelle abandoning him. But now, facing this man, he was glad of the skills he developed.

"Well, I mean, you do remember picking up my wife on the highway?" Victor's eyes bore into him, but the man's smile was like a fixed structure on his face. "I don't mean to imply I am upset with you. In fact, I am upset with myself for the way I acted that day with Lori. And I really need to try to make it up to her. But the thing is I can't find her. She hasn't been back to her home, and you can understand that I am necessarily concerned."

Shay looked right into the man's eyes. There was no sincerity there. The anger and challenge in those eyes made Shay's heart speed up. He felt his hands involuntarily curl into fists. But he stayed in character. He was someone who'd only met Lori briefly.

"Well, I'm glad there are no hard feelings," Shay said. "I was just giving what looked like a lady in distress a ride."

"And I appreciate that," Victor said. "In other circumstances, I would like to think I'd do the same thing myself. But what I really need to know is where you took her?" He spoke in a calm, even voice. His question carefully framed as a plea rather than a command.

"Actually, a restaurant in Red Hall. The KFC," Shay said. "I think I might still have the receipt in my wallet. I bought her lunch."

Shay took out his wallet, opened it, fished around and handed Victor the receipt. "I think the address is on it."

Victor looked over the receipt. "You haven't seen her since then?" Now there was an edge to his voice. A vailed threat behind the words.

"Why would I see her? I dropped her off and bought her lunch because she seemed upset, and I was hungry, and it didn't seem right to just go and eat in front of her.

"In fact, she was filling out an application as I left."

Shay felt Victor studying him. Then Victor glanced at the receipt in his hand with a look of contempt on his face. Shay felt like there was an explosion coming. Where was Deputy Doyle and the state police?

"Then what the hell was her waitress uniform doing in your damn laundry room?" Victor demanded so loudly, Issy looked up in shock from the pile of mail.

"We stopped here. She needed a change of clothes. I let her take some items from our lost and found, and she left the uniform here. I don't know if she intends to come back for it or not." Shay felt his whole body shaking. His mouth was dry. Not since he'd caught Houlihan in bed with his wife, and they'd nearly come to blows had he felt so threatened. "If you'd like to take the uniform with you, that would be fine. You are more likely to see her than we are."

Victor glared at him for a moment, then turned and stormed out the door.

CHAPTER 29: VICTOR

June 30, 2022: 3:04 p.m.

In his room, Victor threw the receipt Shay had given him into the metal waste-basket, then kicked the basket with his right foot. The basket flew across the room where it made a metallic crunch as it hit the bed frame.

As a reward, an intense, dull pain ran like a wave into his right shin between the straps on his brace. Out the glass doors at the back of the room, the clouds seemed to swirl angrily over the mountain. It was precisely how Victor felt. He was sure the bastard was lying. But why? Had Lori asked him to lie?

It made sense she'd try for a job in a restaurant. But there was something wrong. He just knew it.

Think.

If she got the job, maybe she'd be working there already. He walked over to the dented wastebasket and fished out the crumpled receipt. The phone number of the restaurant was on it.

He listened to the ring on the other end of the phone. "You've reached the KFC. How may I help you today?" a female voice asked.

"May I speak to Lori Mysek, please?" Victor asked, making his voice sound as calm and friendly as he could.

There was a pause at the other end of the line. "Is she a customer? There are actually only two customers in the restaurant currently, and they are a man and his little boy."

"No," Victor said. "I was told she was working there now?"

"Well, I'm the assistant manager and I don't know of any Lori Mysek working here."

"I thought she filled out an application?"

"We haven't had any applications turned in lately. Although, if she is seeking employment, I'd be happy to interview her. We are shorthanded."

The woman started to say something else, but Victor slammed the phone down so hard, there was a sharp crack as the plastic in the handset split. He imagined himself storming back to the motel office, pulling that damn meddling asshole who picked up his wife out from behind the desk and beating him to death.

But, instead, he forced himself to calm down.

Think.

Looking down at the receipt that was still in his hand, he noticed that there were three dinners on it, not just two.

CHAPTER 30: ISSY

June 30, 2022: 3:26 p.m.

The office phone rang. Issy answered and then listened.

"Okay," she said.

"Who was that?" Shay asked.

"Deputy Doyle, he call. Police delayed. Big accident I-90. He say to stay away from bad man. Go about business."

Shay nodded. Issy could tell by the look on his face he did not want to wait. And guessed he was worried about Lori.

"Me, I better clean rooms," she said as cheerfully as she could.

"Be careful," Shay said.

There were only 3 rooms left to clean, and as Issy walked out of the first she found Victor Bleché standing in her way.

Her whole body tensed.

"May I help you?" she asked, forcing a smile.

"Yeah," Victor said, smiling himself. "I'm wondering what is down the road that way?"

Issy looked where he was pointing. Although she assumed he meant the road, his finger was pointing in the direction of her trailer. Her mouth went dry. It took her a moment to speak. "Just woods, I be thinking."

"Is there a way out that way?" Victor asked. "Back to the highway, that is?"

Issy nodded. "That be a long way to go, but they be roads that way." Her mouth felt like it was filled with cotton.

She was aware that Victor was staring at her intently. Her heart began to pound in her chest.

"Thank you," Victor said. He turned and began to walk toward his SUV, which was parked about 30 feet away.

Issy's instinct was to run to the office and warn Shay. But she realized that if Victor saw her running to the office, he might suspect something was up and resort to violence to find out what.

Taking the handle of her supply cart, she walked calmly to the next room that needed cleaning just a few doors down. Opening it with her master key, she pushed her cart inside as she heard Victor's vehicle start up.

It was her habit to leave a room door open while she was inside cleaning and though she really wanted to shut the door behind her, she left the door open. She walked to the back of the room and picked up the wastebasket from the bathroom. As she stepped out of the bathroom, she saw Victor's Explorer heading down the road in the direction of her trailer.

Maybe that man just going for a ride, she thought. But deep down, she felt Lori was in danger.

Picking up the phone, she dialed 0'.

"You've reached the Hamilton Hurricane Motel," Shay's voice said cheerfully. "We are not at the desk right now, but if you leave a message, we will get right back to you."

Issy wanted to curse the phone.

"Why you not be there," she cried after the beep. "Dat man go down road wrong way. I am going to walk over through the woods. Make sure that Lori be okay.

CHAPTER 31:
VICTOR

June 30, 2022: 4:08 p.m.

Victor made the turn into the driveway he'd entered earlier and drove up the track to the trailer. As he pulled up in front, he saw a curtain in the front window move. Someone was inside. Someone had heard him drive in and had peeked out. He was pretty sure by the way the cleaning woman at the motel had acted that he knew who that someone was.

Getting out of the car, he took the steps up to the trailer door, two at a time.

Just in case he was wrong, his first knocks were light.

Victor listened. There were no sounds from the trailer.

He knocked again—this time a bit more loudly.

"Hello?" he called. "Anyone home."

The only sounds were the caws of some blue jays in the trees surrounding him.

The trailer, itself, was silent. Victor listened for the sound of any approaching vehicles. Still, the only sounds were that of the birds.

"Lori," Victor cried as loudly as he could. "I know you are in there. And you better damn well come out if you know what is good for you."

It seemed like the trailer shook. The birds stopped chattering.

The cozy little grotto the trailer was nested in fell into shadow as a cloud passed overhead. Victor stepped back and kicked in the door.

CHAPTER 32: LORI

June 30: 2022: 4:08 p.m.

When Lori heard a vehicle pull up the driveway, she hoped it was Shay.

She had been in the living room, reading and drinking tea.

A quick tour of the trailer when she arrived had revealed a kitchen, a bedroom dominated more by a computer set-up with three monitors than the bed, a room filled with boxes, a bathroom with a tub with a shower door and the inviting living room.

Lori had gravitated toward the living room, decorated with Jamaican art, colorful pillows, and a painting of a man with long dreadlocks that Lori did not recognize.

No television was in evidence. Lori realized as she sunk into the soft couch how tiring the trip to find Harper had been.

But she had been sitting for some time and had been thinking of getting up anyway, when she heard the vehicle. Lori lifted a corner of the lace curtain on the partly open window closest to her and peeked out.

She felt her stomach drop. Her heart began to beat wildly. She suddenly couldn't move. She watched frozen as Victor rose from the Explorer and turned toward the trailer.

She managed to let the curtain fall; she could almost feel Victor staring at the window. Had he seen the curtain move?

Luckily, she had not had to turn any lights on in order to be able to read. Walking quickly, she went to the kitchen. From a wooden block of knives, she gasped the biggest knife and pulled it out. Through the partly open front window, she could hear the crunch of gravel as Victor headed for the trailer's only door. Lori looked down at the knife in her hand. In a physical education class at the University of Montana, a teacher had talked briefly one day about self-defense. They wouldn't touch on self-defense in this basic Phys-ed course, but the teacher suggested such courses as a good way to stay in shape. One thing the teacher did mention was that knives were not very good protection. A person stronger than you would always be able to use your knife against you.

She started to put the knife down, but then decided to keep it.

She had to hide. She was moving across the living room toward the hallway to the bedroom when the door burst open.

She ran toward the bedroom, hoping to bar the door. Victor was after her in a flash. At the bedroom door, she stumbled. The knife twisted as her hand hit the doorway. As she fell onto the bedroom floor, the knife dug into her side.

She looked down at the blood seeping out of her as Victor's hands grabbed her.

CHAPTER 33: ISSY

June 30, 2022, 4:34 p.m.

Issy was 50 yards away from the trailer when she heard a vehicle start up. A stand of lodgepole blocked her view. Issy began to run. There was no reason for a car to be in her driveway. From time to time, she had worried about thieves breaking in and stealing her computer equipment. But in her heart, she knew this was about Lori.

When she emerged from the trees, she heard a vehicle speeding away on the road. Looking across her yard, she could see the trailer's door hanging askew.

Running to the trailer, Issy rushed inside. The lights were off, and parts of her home were in shadow. The living room and kitchen were empty. Aside from the broken door, nothing else seemed amiss. Her heart beating, she moved, toward the back of the trailer. By her bedroom door, light coming in the window illuminated a dark red pool of something on the carpet.

The bedroom seemed empty. She felt sick as she bent down and touched the dark stain. It was warm. She lifted a finger covered in blood.

She flicked the hall lights on. A bloody kitchen knife, one of hers, lay on the carpet a few feet away from the large bloodstain.

Looking around, she noticed smaller drops of blood led down the hallway. They ran from tiny droplets to tennis ball sized stains. In the bathroom, there was a puddle of blood just inside the door.

Bloody fingerprints covered the wall by the empty toilet

paper holder.

Bloody smears streaked the bathroom sink.

She followed the bloodstains to the broken door.

Bile rose in her throat. Droplets of blood had fallen on the steps.

For a moment, her vision went dark. She fought to pull herself together. Now was not the time to faint.

She had trouble keeping her balance as she made her way to the phone on the kitchen wall.

"Shay, he has her. And I think he cut her," she cried into the phone when, to her relief, Shay answered.

CHAPTER 34: WINSLOW

June 30, 2022: 6:51 p.m.

Winslow stood in the motel's driveway. He sighed and looked off at the mountains. Shay Hamilton and Issy Wint looked at him expectantly.

"I am deeply sorry that I couldn't get here sooner.

"Anyway, the crime scene team is processing the trailer. We already had a bolo on this Victor Bleché's car. If any officers or traffic cams spot it, we will know immediately."

There were only three vehicles left in the motel parking lot. Issy, who had been looking at the vehicles, pointed to a plate on the single truck there. "That be not the right plate," Issy said.

Winslow checked. The plate on the truck was the one that should have been on Victor's SUV.

"You've got a good eye," Winslow said.

When he'd finished calling the plate switch in, he said, "Let's go inside. I've a few things to say."

In the motel office, Winslow looked from one to the other. "I did check out the blood in the room. It is disturbing, but it is not enough blood to indicate that whoever was stabbed lost so much as to be in real danger. But that person could be bleeding inside. It would depend on where the injury occurred. We also do not know who stabbed who? Until the crime techs finish, we won't know. We have Victor's Blood type from the prison records. He needed a transfusion when his leg was broken. We can always hope the blood is his.

"But would Lori drive him away if he was the one injured?" Issy asked.

Winslow nodded. "He'd have to have forced her. Maybe at gunpoint."

CHAPTER 35: LORI

July 1, 2022: 9:03 a.m.

As Lori woke, she saw spider webs--holding dust—swaying above her. She noticed slender, cave-like cracks in the soft brown logs of a wall. By the closed wooden door, a bright shaft of sunlight from a skylight gleamed off a broom handle. There was a faint scent of woodsmoke. She heard a rhythmic clunking. Turning her head, she saw a slowing fan, atop a glass-fronted wood stove, was making that noise. From inside the stove, tiny red embers seemed to watch her like eyes. It was very warm in the room.

Where was she? She was lying down on some kind of bed. She shifted her body. Blinding. burning pain shot through her lower-right side.

She tried to fight the pain.

Focus on something else. She tried to concentrate on a spiderweb that was hanging between two rafters directly above her. With her right hand, she reached down to where the pain was emanating. There was a blanket there. She felt her way under the blanket. Fire raged through her lower body as she touched threads encrusted with something hard and flaky. Moving her hand, she felt beneath her.

Then it all came flooding back. Running from Victor in the double-wide. Carrying the knife. "Never run with a knife in your hand." Was that the saying. Or was it scissors? She had fallen on the knife as she tried to get away.

And that was all she could remember.

She glanced around her now. Log walls formed a roomy

box around her. There was the wood stove with a glass door, but the fire was definitely going out.

She tried to lift herself up, and the wave of pain was like two halves of her side were splitting apart.

A black mist seemed to grow around her. She lay back down. Her head swimming. Where was she? Where was Victor?

"Hello?" she cried.

The only sound that came in answer was a scurrying of something like a small creature in a corner behind her head. After what happened the last time she tried to move, she lay still. It's just a mouse, she told herself.

"Victor?" She called. Her throat was dry. Her voice sounded feeble.

"Victor!" She yelled as loud as she dared, the effort causing more pain than she imagined.

But there was no reply. Had he gone? If so, where was he?

She could move her hands. Carefully and slowly, she tried to move her legs. First the right. She could move it. Then the left. She could move it too.

She wasn't tied down. Had he locked her in this cabin? As far as she could tell, it was only one room. The windows seemed intact.

If he was gone, this was her chance to escape. She tried lifting herself from the bed again. The pain stabbed into her side, but not as intensely as it had before. Fighting a sense of darkness that seemed to sweep over her, she forced herself to sit up.

The room swirled around her. She felt her balance tilt. She almost couldn't sit upright on what she now realized was a cot.

Her side ached. The blanket on her lap slid off. With slow fingers, she reached down and touched her side again.

She winced as her fingertips touched her wound. Yes, there were stitches. Had Victor sewn her up?

She looked around. From where she sat, there was only one small window in the three walls she could see.

She was alone. This might be her only chance to get away.

She leaned forward.

A bolt of hot fire radiated from her side and she cried out. Steeling herself, she pushed down on her legs and forced herself to stand.

A wave of darkness circled her. Her side felt like a thousand knives piercing her. But she managed to stay on her feet somehow.

She moved her left foot a few inches. It hurt, but the pain was bearable. She hesitated. She knew moving her right foot was going to hurt more. Clenching her teeth, she took a step. The black wave washed over her again. But it cleared.

Put the pain out of your mind, she told herself.

She moved her left foot. She moved her right foot. The blackness tried to come in, but she pushed it away. She made the pain in her side belong to someone else. Someone she was observing.

It seemed to take forever but finally, she was at what appeared to be a handmade door. Instead of a knob, it had a latch. Tentatively, she reached for the latch. The effort sent a new bolt of pain through her.

Would Victor be outside?

CHAPTER 36:
VICTOR

July 1, 2022: 8:50 a.m.

The small drug store smelled like flowers and bandages. Fluorescent lights lit aisles filled with everything from diapers to women's cosmetics.

A short man wearing a white lab coat, his trim beard speckled with gray, was busy doing something in the pharmacy at the far end of the store.

"How may I help you, sir?" The man asked as Victor stepped up to the counter.

"I have a friend who has a bad cut. And I don't know what I need to do to fix it."

"How deep is the cut?"

"Pretty deep. She fell on a knife and cut herself here," Victor said, pointing to his side just above his hip."

"Did you take her to the hospital?" the pharmacist asked anxiously, his eyes looking into Victor's.

"It isn't that bad, and she is stubborn. But I'd like to try and make sure it doesn't get infected."

The man's blue eyes showed concern. "How long is the cut?"

"About this long," Victor said, spreading the fingers of his hand about four inches apart.

"Can you help me?"

"And how deep did the knife go in?" the man asked. This time, there was something about the way he asked the question that Victor did not like.

"Well," Victor said. "She didn't fall on the point, thank God. She fell onto the side of it, and I'd say in went in an inch or so."

The man's eyes showed alarm. "Sir, you need to take your friend to the hospital. At the very least, she'd need stitches with a cut that long and deep. And antibiotics."

"The problem is she's a member of this weird religious group, Christ's something or other, and she doesn't believe in doctors."

After a moment, the man nodded. "Come on and let's see what we have on the isles that you can use."

After about ten minutes Victor had an armload of bandages, topical antibiotics, gauze rolls, medical tape, alcohol pads, and medical gloves.

"Can I get some pain meds for her?" Victor asked.

"Well, you can get Motrin. That usually works pretty well. But most of those religious groups that don't believe in hospitals won't take anything."

Before the pharmacist could react, Victor lifted himself onto the counter like a gymnast mounting a sawhorse, swung his legs around, and dropped down next to the startled pharmacist. He pulled his knife from behind his back. "I need something stronger than Motrin. I want Oxy or Hydrocodone."

"Hey, I'd love to help you. And I feel for you. But if you don't put that knife away and leave right now, you are going to be in big trouble."

"Don't you know not to mess with a man who has nothing left to lose?"

The terrified man just stared at Victor.

"Oh, and I'll need antibiotics!" Victor didn't say anything more. He just moved the knife a little closer to the man and gave him a look he'd perfected in prison.

Minutes later, as Victor walked out of the store, the pharmacist picked up the store's phone with a shaking hand.

CHAPTER 37: WINSLOW

July 1, 2022: 7:06 a.m.

Shay, Issy, and Winslow sat at the breakfast table in Shay's office apartment. Shay had invited Winslow to stay at the motel as his guest. Winslow had accepted Shay's invitation because the motel was a more central location than his mountain cabin. All had finished eating, and Shay and Issy sipped coffee as Winslow spoke on his cell phone.

As Winslow pocketed his phone, his expression was grim. "A man fitting Victor's description just held up a pharmacy in Deer Lodge. He took bandages, other first aid equipment, penicillin, and Hydrocodone."

Winslow knew he wasn't supposed to share case info but decided that it would be better not to spare these people what was obvious. He was only a part-time deputy and handling the feelings of victims' friends and family was not something he had a great deal of experience with.

"The man himself did not appear injured. It would seem that Lori was the one stabbed."

"My God!" Issy cried.

"But we know she is still alive," Shay said.

"Well," Winslow was somber. "We know she was alive when he left her. How badly she is wounded we don't know. We don't know if she is restrained or simply locked in wherever he is keeping her. There is a possibility that she could escape while he is gone. But likewise, it is possible that she is badly wounded, and if she tries to get away, she will be worse off than if she stayed put.

"But where could he have taken her?" Issy asked.

"We don't know. My boss set up a meeting with Victor's cellmate in Deer Lodge." looking down at the watch Shawna, his fiancée, had given him, he added, "In fact, I need to get going now.

"Thank you for letting me stay here. It's going to make getting to the prison a lot easier."

As Winslow rose to go, Issy asked, "What's the cellmate's name?"

Winslow hesitated and gave her a questioning look.

"I'm pretty good with a computer. If Victor is close enough to go to a pharmacy in Deer Lodge, wherever he took her is in this area. I can do a search for properties in the man's name," Issy explained.

Winslow nodded. His name is John Cristy Feldor. His nickname is 'Bozo' if that helps at all."

Issy nodded.

CHAPTER 38: LORI

July 1, 2022: 9:34 a.m.

Lori steadied herself against the door as the wave of pain washed through her. The wood was cool beneath her fingers. For the moment, she concentrated on holding herself upright as darkness seemed to swim around her eyes.

Don't faint. I can't let myself faint.

Had Victor locked the door. With one hand still on the door, she put her fingers on the cold metal latch and lifted. The bar that held the door to the frame lifted.

She eased herself back from the door.

Lori's heart beat wildly as she gave the door a little tug. The door didn't move. It was stuck. Lori's heart sank. Lori tried pulling harder. Her side began to scream. Then, suddenly, the door popped open an inch, letting in the sunlight.

She stepped back, gave the latch a further pull, and the door swung open wide.

Not 10 yards in front of her were a thick copse of trees. Lodgepole and a giant larch. There was no yard to speak of, just small plants growing out of the cleared soil around the cabin.

Lori looked left and right. No driveway. No road. Just a path ambling to her left from the door of the cabin.

Lori stepped across the doorway. A wave of dizziness sent her off balance. She grabbed the door frame and hung on. When the darkness ebbed, she let go of the doorframe and stepped, tentatively, down to the dirt path that veered to the left.

She looked ahead into the forest. *Please don't let me run*

into him, she pleaded. She took a step and then turned back. She'd left the door open.

Bending as she reached for it tore at her side. She fought the black cloud that threatened to blind her. She pulled the door shut. Luckily, the latch caught.

She backed away from the door. It seemed hard to lift her feet.

She began sliding them along the path, pushing tiny branches and pine needles up as she moved forward.

At the edge of the clearing, she turned back, realizing she hadn't really checked around the cabin to see if there was a driveway on the other side. But as far as she could see, there was no sign of a path on either side of the cabin.

She needed to find a road. She needed to find someone who could help her.

The path weaved through the forest. Plants rose between the bases of the trees. The air felt cool. Her side burned. At times, the trail went straight ahead for 20 or 30 feet, and then it would swing around a tree or giant clump of brush. All the while she walked, she kept looking to her sides. She knew she would need a place to hide if Victor came back. Would she be able to hear him? Would she even have time to hide?

Then, up ahead, there seemed to be more light coming through the pines. Was she nearing the end of the maze of trees that shrouded the path?

She quickened her pace, feeling a sharp stabbing in her side for the effort. Finally, she broke through into the meadow. The meadow was empty. There were ruts where a vehicle had pulled in and stopped near the path. But the vehicle was not here now. The tire tracks ran out to the edge of the meadow, then swung around a row of trees. That was where the road had to be.

She slipped on soft mud and stumbled as she stepped onto one of the tracks. Mud oozed up around her shoes. She stepped over to the grass. The earth was soft beneath the grass, but not as bad as the muddy tracks.

She made a beeline for the line of trees.

Her heart lifted as she slipped through the trees. On the other side of the trees, the muddy driveway turned into a packed dirt road.

Lori listened. There were no vehicle sounds. She guessed what she was looking at was a wilderness road that was used primarily by hunters. Who would want to live out here?

The question was: Which way should she go? The road stretched to her left and her right. She appeared to be in a deep gulch. She had no idea what time it was, so the position of the sun didn't help. She had no idea which direction was North, South, East, or West.

If she picked the wrong direction, Victor could come driving up and spot her walking. But then, she shook her head. If she went away from the direction Victor was coming from, she would be going further into the woods, farther away from any possible help. Without help, could she even survive?

She could hear the sound of a stream on the other side of the road. She moved toward it, and somehow managed to suppress the pain as she got down on her hands and knees and drank deeply. When she satisfied her thirst, she moved back to the road.

Left, or right? That was the decision she had to make. And it could be a life-threatening decision.

Despair seemed to come up like a cloud around her, the world itself felt against her. The sun at that moment went behind a cloud and the gulch darkened. She looked up toward the sun now hidden by the clouds and saw in the bright pink and yellow halo the sun made of the cloud a rift of bright light as if the sun were breaking through. "Oh, Lord help me," Lori whispered. And then, and it seemed almost a miracle, an idea came to her.

CHAPTER 39: WINSLOW

July 1, 2022: 8:35 a.m.

Winslow sat on a bolted down bench with his hands on the metal table in front of him. His weapon was securely locked away in the guard house. And the only thing on the table was a large book laying facedown. In the center of the table was a large iron loop for handcuffing the men who were to be interviewed. A door on the opposite side of the bench opened, and a uniformed guard stepped through. Behind him, a skinny man about six feet tall, with a tonsured head and a day's growth of beard, followed. Behind that man, another, even taller guard stood; the man was even taller than Winslow.

"Do you want him locked up?" The first guard whose name tag read 'WALSH' asked.

"No," Winslow said. "I don't need him handcuffed. As long as you frisked him."

The guard gave Winslow an annoyed look and then turned to the prisoner. "Turn to the wall and assume the position!"

When the prisoner had been searched and the deputies had left, Winslow stood and offered his hand.

"I'm Winslow Doyle. I'd like to ask you about your former cellmate, Victor Bleché."

The prisoner's eyes were red. He stared directly into Winslow's eyes with a defiance only someone who had nothing left to lose could achieve.

Winslow noted the man was clenching and unclenching his fingers.

"Don't know nothing about 'em," Bozo said. But the man's eyes had drifted to the book on the table.

"Well, I just thought you might know where in the area he might hang out?" Winslow asked.

"He's nothing to me," Bozo said. His eyes lifted from the book and again stared directly into Winslow's.

Winslow had expected this. He looked around the room as if to see if he were being watched. Then opened the book to a random page. A full Color photo of Miss July 1977 appeared for a moment, and then Winslow shut the book so fast it slapped closed.

"That's too bad," Winslow said.

"If I tell you, you give me that book?" Bozo asked.

Winslow nodded.

"I got a place not that far from here..." Bozo began, "It's listed under my mother's maiden name, so nobody knows the property is mine. It's a little hard to find, but I can give you directions."

CHAPTER 40: ISSY

July 1, 2022: 9:03 a.m.

They'd had to wait until the crime scene team had processed Issy's trailer before they could go in.

Now, Shay paced back and forth behind Issy, who was working at her computer bank.

"I know you're upset, boss, but your moving around is distracting me."

"Do you have anything yet?" Shay asked, impatiently.

"Well, they be nothing under this guy's name. But I check his name on an ancestry website. Some sister of his make a family tree.

"Now, I look under his mama's birth name."

A few minutes later, she threw her hands up. "Found it!"

Shay looked at the screen. There was a listing for Emma Waitheart, a 20 acre parcel up Bear Gulch.

"Good job," Shay said, patting Issy's shoulders.

A few moments later, Issy had found a map on Google Earth with a pin in the location of Bozo's mother's cabin. Shay had hunted in that area and knew exactly where it was.

"Got it," Shay said.

As Shay rushed out the door, Issy called after him. "Hey boss, I check…"

But Shay must not have heard her, because the door slammed. Moments later, she heard Shay's truck pull away from the trailer.

"The big picture," Issy said to herself. "Or little picture."

On the screen, Issy zoomed in on the area where the pin

was pointing. The image increased dramatically. Issy knew there would be no street view on a dirt road in the wilderness, but she might be able to learn something that would help Shay by getting a more detailed view of the property.

When the program had zoomed down to as close as it could get without a street view, Issy gasped.

She fumbled taking out her phone, and it clattered to the floor. Hurriedly, she picked it up. It took three tries to press the button that would speed dial Shay.

CHAPTER 41: VICTOR

July 1, 2022: 10:48 a.m.

Victor hurried along the path to the cabin. He had the supplies he'd stolen from the pharmacy in his hands. His heart beat like a drum roll. Would Lori be alright? She hadn't looked good when he'd left.

He burst through the cabin door and stopped. Lori was not on the cot he'd set up for her.

He looked around the room wild-eyed. Where was she?

He put the packages he was carrying on the floor.

Maybe she had to pee? He slapped his head. He hadn't thought to bring in a slop bucket for her. He turned to the door, which hung open. His eyes went to the floor. There were fresh drops of blood.

Following the drops, he saw quickly that they did not lead to the outhouse, which was in the back of the cabin, but rather down the trail to where he'd parked his Explorer. He thought for a moment of going back in for the bandages. She was bleeding again. How bad he did not know. Then he realized he'd left the keys in the Explorer.

He forced himself to run as best he could.

CHAPTER 42: LORI

July 1, 2022: 10:23 a.m.

Crouched down behind some trees by the spot where Victor had been parked, Lori fought to stay awake. The pain for the moment had died to a dull ache, that only flared if she moved. So, she didn't move. But her body felt so tired, she kept feeling she was dozing off. She just hoped she'd be awake and able to move when Victor got back.

She knew where he hid his keys. When she lived with him, he always put his keys inside the flap of his gas tank. She had thought that a smart crook would look there, but the car was never stolen. That, of course, did not mean he had been right.

She heard the car before she saw it. Instantly on alert, she looked toward the line of trees around which the dirt track swung.

Hidden behind a tangle of branches, there was space enough for her to see out. If it were someone else, she would signal them and be rescued.

Her heart began to beat, as she recognized Victor's Ford Explorer.

Victor was driving very fast. The car screeched to a stop, the door swung open, and Victor jumped out. Pausing only to shut the door, Victor rushed down the trail toward the cabin.

Lori tried to stand. Her pain roared and she stumbled. She knew the hard part in getting to the car and getting away would be her ability to move fast enough.

She needed time to get to the SUV. Get the key from the hidden compartment, get in the car, start it, and drive off.

She thought of Victor going toward the cabin as fast as he could. Why was he hurrying? Was he thinking she'd escape?

She had to ignore the pain. Stepping between the branches of the fallen tree she'd hidden behind; she caught her shirt on the gnarled fingers of a branch. She lost precious moments untangling herself. When she stepped free of the tree, she forced herself to walk as quickly as her pain allowed. The long strides tore at her side, but she focused on the SUV.

She had to dig down for each breath as it felt like she could not get enough air. As she reached the SUV, she crashed against it.

She began falling. She threw her hand out and grabbed the roof. It stopped her fall, but a wave of pain made her bend over.

Bent, she could see through the passenger side window Victor had left the keys in the ignition.

Leaning forward, she slid her hands to the hood and began to take small steps. Her side, in addition to the pain, felt wet. Was she bleeding? Balancing on the hood, she rounded the front of the vehicle.

From down the trail, she heard the familiar voice cry out loudly, "Lori!"

Victor had parked by the grass, and on the driver's side the clumps of grass were hard to walk on. She tried to push herself faster, but her body would not respond. It seemed to her she was moving in slow motion.

Finally, she reached the edge of the door. With her hands on the roof she moved far enough over to reach the handle.

"Lori?" The voice called again. This time much closer.

Lori opened the door and leaned in, putting her left hand on the roof above the driver's seat.

Lifting her right leg sent waves of pain through her right side. Shifting her butt onto the seat caused another wave of pain.

It was then that she looked up and saw Victor emerge into the clearing from the path. She saw the look on his face change from concern to rage. He had been hobbling along steadily, but now he picked up his gait.

As she swung her left foot into the vehicle, a black cloud caused by a shooting peak of pain almost obscured her vision. She fought it. It cleared. She grabbed the key in the ignition and as she did so, managed to turn it.

The engine roared to life.

Out the front window, Victor was only yards away. The driver's side door hung wide open, and there was no way she could reach it and close it. There was no time to fuss with her seat belt.

Victor's right hand closed on the open door.

Lori put the Explorer in reverse and stepped on the gas.

As the car lurched backward, Victor was pulled off his feet. She kept the gas pedal down, the tires gripped, then skidded a bit on the grass. She did not want to get stuck.

For a moment or two, Victor held on to the door. Finally, his hand let go. He fell and rolled.

Lori swung the wheel in a turn. The movement swung the driver's door closed.

Then the car stopped moving. The tires screamed. Victor rose, looked at her. Shouted something she could not hear over the squeal of the tires.

Then he was moving toward her.

She had to think. She took her foot off the gas. Took the SUV out of reverse and put it into drive. Victor had reached the door. His hand went to the handle.

Lori stepped on the gas.

Even above the engine, she could hear Victor scream as his hand caught in the door handle, and he was pulled along.

She didn't see him fall free but could feel the difference in the way the Explorer lurched forward as it freed itself of Victor's weight. She glanced in the rearview mirror and saw him lying on the ground, holding his arm. Then she swung around the line of trees and Victor was out of sight.

By the time she reached the intersection of the dirt

trail with the main road, the blackness was threatening to overwhelm her again.

She slowed for a moment and pulled on her seat belt.

Now, she had the same dilemma she had before while on foot.

Which way did she need to turn to get back to the highway and help?

Instinct told her to turn left. But she didn't trust her instinct. After marrying Victor and getting pregnant by Jeffery, she didn't trust her instinct at all. She turned right.

The packed dirt road she followed wound upward between large monoliths of gray and brown stone. She looked at her pants leg. It was dark with her blood. The wound had opened up and was bleeding freely now. As she topped a rise and rushed downward, a tunnel of black narrowed her view.

Suddenly, she realized, she was going the wrong way. She had taken a drink from the stream. The water was going in the opposite direction. Somewhere in her past, she'd heard you always follow the water downstream to find civilization. She'd gone the wrong way.

Just as she was about to slow to turn around, the black tunnel narrowed to just a spec of light before her.

She was losing consciousness.

CHAPTER 43: SHAY

July 1, 2022: 10:03 a.m.

Shay pulled up in front of a heavily overgrown roadway. Tangles of young willow crisscrossed in front of the track. A few feet in, a stream gurgled. There was no way to enter the driveway. Shay pulled to the side of the road. Was this it?

He looked down at the GPS he'd bought to search for Harper.

This was the right location.

He startled when he heard a vehicle on the road behind him. He stepped back behind his truck and put his hand on the butt of his gun.

To his relief, Winslow Doyle's Jeep appeared, a beacon--a portable light bar--beaming from the Jeep's roof.

Doyle pulled up behind Shay's truck.

"How did you get here?" Deputy Doyle asked. Doyle's eyes going to the revolver strapped to Shay's side.

"My office assistant, Issy, is good with computers. She looked up properties belonging to Feldor's relatives in the area. This is the only one."

"I take it you just got here?" Doyle asked.

"Yes, sir."

Winslow walked back to the dirt track blocked by willows and examined the ground around the spring. "It doesn't look like anyone's walked in this way. They certainly didn't drive in. Let me call for backup just in case."

"We haven't got time for backup," Shay said. "He could kill her." And, stepping through the willows, began to walk up the overgrown drive.

He expected the deputy to call out, order hint to stop. Instead, he heard the deputy follow.

.

Seven minutes later, Shay stopped and stared at the collapsed building in front of him.

"Nobody is staying here," Winslow said behind him.

Shay's heart had been beating fast on the walk-up. Now his whole body felt tired. "Then where can they be?" he said. His desperation evident in his tone.

They were on their way back to their vehicles when Shay's cell phone pinged.

As he took out his phone, he said, "I can't believe I got a signal here."

"You never know in the wilderness," Winslow said. "You get spots in different places where your phone suddenly works."

Shay held the phone out to Winslow. "Seems I missed Issy's message about this place. She found it on Google Earth just after I left and could see it was in ruins.

"But she did find three places nearby where Victor Bleché could have brought Lori."

The first two cabins were nearby and were both within yards of the road. A quick check had shown no signs of recent occupation.

The third place was off the road. And Shay realized it was a much more likely place for Victor to hide.

They parked in a meadow. Tracks indicated that at least one vehicle had been in and out recently.

As Shay exited his truck, Winslow Doyle held his index finger to his lips in what Shay realized meant they needed to be quiet.

Shay started to turn to shut his truck's door, and Winslow shook his head. The deputy's driver's door was also open.

The deputy eased his door shut, making as little sound as

possible.

Shay understood. He eased his own door shut.

Doyle motioned for Shay to come toward him.

"There is blood on the grass here," Doyle whispered in Shay's ear.

Shay's heart raced.

"There appears to be a trail going that way," Doyle said, pointing.

"Follow me a few steps back," Doyle ordered.

Shay felt almost faint as Doyle led the way along what was, obviously, a well-worn path. On the plants and stones, Shay could see red drops of blood.

Moments later, they came to a clearing in which a small cabin had been built.

Winslow leaned close to Shay's ear. "Stay here and cover the door. I am going to walk around and see if there is another exit."

Shay studied the cabin. The window by the door was too narrow for a person to sneak out of. Shay knew some people made windows small like that, so bears couldn't break in.

As he waited for Doyle, Shay felt faint. At any moment, Victor Bleché might appear, and it would be up to Shay to stop him.

Time slowed. Shay tried to slow his beating heart by taking deep breaths and exhaling slowly. Don't panic!

Then, finally, Doyle appeared from the other side of the cabin.

The deputy began moving toward the door of the cabin. He waved Shay over.

At the door, Doyle whispered in Shay's ear, "Stand to the side of the door. If I'm shot, do not try to follow me. Go "back to my Jeep and radio for backup."

Shay nodded.

Doyle stood full in front of the door and with his right

foot kicked the door in. The deputy's body followed in almost the same movement.

As Shay leaned against the wall. His whole body was shaking.

"Clear," Deputy Doyle called from inside.

Shay stared at the drops of blood spread wide across the floor. His eyes went to a cot, on which lay a bloody blanket.

Doyle was spreading open a plastic pharmacy bag on the kitchen table, revealing unopened packages of bandages and other first aid supplies.

"He went to get something to bandage her, and she left while he was gone?" Shay asked.

"That's what I'm thinking," Winslow said. "We need to go back to where our cars are parked. I didn't see any traces of blood when I walked around the cabin. So, she went out via that path. Maybe we can track her.

Deputy Doyle had Shay stand by their vehicles while he searched for tracks and other signs. Finally, Doyle waved Shay over to a spot just in the trees about 50 feet from where the path to the cabin began.

"She hid here. I think she waited for him to come back and then stole his SUV.

"But we didn't pass her?" Shay said.

"No, which means she went the other way."

"But where is Victor if he doesn't have a vehicle?"

CHAPTER 44:
VICTOR

July 1, 2022: 10:59 a.m.

Victor had just pulled himself up from where he had fallen when he heard what sounded like a metallic crunch far beyond the trees to his left. The sound was immediately followed by the very loud wail of a car horn.

She'd crashed. She'd been too weak and lost control. That he could hear the horn, which was still blasting away, meant she couldn't be too far.

However, sounds in the wilderness traveled funny. Something sounding like it was blocks away could be miles.

He began to run. The sound of the horn died. He had almost reached the turn around the trees when he heard a vehicle coming his way.

He ducked behind a tree and crouched down. Moments later a red Jeep Cherokee with a cop light on the top, appeared, followed a moment later by a Blue Chevy truck. The cop light on the Jeep was not on.

Through the blades of grass in front of him, Victor's eyes went to the truck.

It was the motel guy's truck. The one who'd picked up Lori. Victor felt as if his blood was beginning to boil. He felt a dull pain as if something hard was pressing at his forehead. His fingers clenched into fists.

Think, Victor told himself.

They'd be getting out in a moment. He couldn't risk them

seeing him. With his hands and knees, barely lifting himself off the ground, Victor crawled along the beargrass, mullein, and tiny new pine trees through the border of trees.

The vehicles stopped. He heard car doors open. Victor did not look back. He didn't rise until the stand of trees blocked his view of the vehicles. Then he began hobbling toward the main road.

CHAPTER 45: LORI

July 1, 2022: 11:08 a.m.

A haze seemed to cover her eyes when she first tried to open them. And then, suddenly, her nose hurt. She lifted her right hand to her nose too quickly, and the touch of her hand sent a jolt of pain through her head.

Her hand came back bloody. She could see her hand now. She looked up; memory came flooding back. She was in Victor's Explorer. She had driven away.

The explorer was pointed down into a sort of ditch. An airbag was deflated in her lap. Her side burned. There was a standing tree pressed against the center of the hood. The hood had been crunched slightly in. She'd been driving away from Victor when she blacked out and apparently crashed.

She reached for the ignition key.

"Please start."

The Explorer turned over. She put the SUV in reverse. She could hear the wheels spin. She stepped harder on the gas. The wheels spun louder.

She was stuck. She turned the engine off.

How far had she gotten from Victor? As far as she could remember, she hadn't gotten that far.

What if he was coming? She had to get out and hide.

She pulled the door handle. The handle moved. She could hear the lock click open. But the door wouldn't budge.

She pushed against it. The door didn't move, and her side flared with pain. Summoning up her energy, she hit the door with her left shoulder. Now her bandaged cut screamed. But the door had opened a few inches.

She pushed, and the door opened a few inches more.

She kept pushing, on and off, letting her pain ebb between pushes as she took little rest breaks. Finally, after one hard push, the opening was wide enough for her to slip out. But as she turned to exit the SUV, something held her back. She struggled for a moment, then laughed. She had her seat belt on.

The release fought against her bloody fingers. She wiped her fingers on her blouse. The seat belt released on her next try. She moved the seat belt out of the way and slipped out the door.

Moments later, she was stumbling along as quickly as she could on the packed dirt road away from the cabin. She had thought about making her way through the woods, out of sight, in case Victor came after her. But the idea of making her way through the brush and having to step over the crisscrossing trees that were blown down, seemed impossible.

If she heard someone coming, she would try and enter the woods wherever she was at the moment.

She didn't know how long she'd been walking when she thought she heard footfalls behind her.

She stopped. Turned. The road twisted behind her, and so she could see only so far.

But she could still hear what sounded like someone coming toward her. The sounds were getting nearer.

Her eyes went first to her left. New growth of some sort of pine grew so thick she could not see between the trees. She knew that meant that the area had been logged and that new trees had started to grow.

On her right, there were older trees with some new young trees growing between them. There was room there for her to slip in and hide. She made for those trees.

CHAPTER 46: SHAY

July 1, 2022: 11:02 a.m.

"See, here," Deputy Doyle said, pointing to a spot on the ground where all Shay could see was some scuffing of the grass.

"He must have held on to the car and got dragged. He fell here."

Shay took the man's word for it. He was obviously good at reading tracks.

"So, what do we do?" Shay asked.

"We need to find her first and make sure she's okay," Winslow said. "He can wait. But we have to be careful. Victor Bleché may have been injured when he fell and was dragged, but we don't know how badly. If at all."

Doyle motioned to Shay to come close. "He was here when we got here. Over by the line of trees," he whispered. His tracks lead off back toward the road."

"He went after her?" Shay said aloud. Then caught himself.

"Looks like it," Doyle whispered.

Minutes later, at the main road, Doyle pulled over. Shay pulled up behind him.

Shay watched as Doyle surveyed the roadway.

"There are faint tracks of someone with a bad leg hurrying along here," Doyle said. "Going in the direction she most likely went. Away from the direction we came in."

"How can he expect to catch her?' Shay asked.

"Well, for one thing," Doyle said. "It's pretty hard to find your way through back here. He might be counting on her having to turn around.

"And if she's in bad shape, she might not be able to drive for long."

Winslow's expression was grim. "You follow me," Winslow said.

CHAPTER 47:
VICTOR

July 1, 2022: 11:25 a.m.

His lungs aching, Victor slowed. He was pacing himself. He hobbled along as fast as he could for as long as he could up the hard-packed road. Then he'd stop and walk to catch his breath.

He was walking now up toward the top of the section of road that climbed next to a pillar of stone. To his right, trees rose up a steep incline. A deer he hadn't seen startled and ran off. A smaller deer following moments later.

As he reached a level area at the top of the climb, the road curved. He'd only gone a few steps when he saw the back end of his SUV rising up out of a ditch.

Victor sped up.

The driver's door hung partway open. It was kept from opening further by some branches of willow that grew down in the earth at the edge of the ditch. The hood of the Explorer was a twisted lip of metal rising against a thick tree. The Explorer had obviously hit it with some speed. Victor ran to the driver's door.

There was no sign of Lori inside.

It was then, he saw the blood smeared on the door and the door frame. She had slid out. Bleeding as she did so.

Victor listened, hoping to hear some sound of her. A bird squawked. Some distance away, a stream gurgled. But there was no sound of movement.

"Lori," Victor cried as loudly as he could. "You're hurt. You need help. Yell! Scream! Let me know where you are, so I can help you."

Victor waited. There was no reply.

With nothing else to do, Victor scanned the ground around the Explorer. There was a blood trail on the dirt road. Lori seemed to be listing from side to side as she stumbled along. Victor followed the blood trail.

About 60 yards from where the vehicle crashed, the large stone formations receded. And the forest again brushed up against the roadway.

Not much further on, the blood trail turned off the road into the woods. Victor picked his way carefully between the trees. There seemed to be too much blood.

Stepping over a fat, blown-down tree, Victor's foot came down on Lori's outstretched thigh. She didn't stir.

Grabbing the tree for balance, Victor slipped over the tree and crouched down by her.

Lying against its trunk, hidden from the road, she faced the forest. Her eyes were closed. Her chest rose and fell with shallow breaths.

"Lori," Victor cried.

She did not reply. He knelt down and touched her forehead. She was burning up. At least, thank God, she was still alive.

Carefully, he lifted her bloodstained blouse. The wound beneath the old bandages was oozing blood, not badly, but steadily.

Victor cursed himself for not bringing the bandages. He began unbuttoning his shirt, intending to use it to bandage her, when he heard vehicles on the road.

Victor listened.

The vehicles stopped. Although they were out of sight, he knew they had stopped by the wreck. And it was a pretty good guess it was the two he'd seen in the meadow.

The faint sound of two men talking carried to him, but he couldn't tell what they were saying.

That meant they'd be following the blood trail shortly.

Victor looked down at Lori. "I am sorry." He bent down and kissed her on the forehead. "I wanted you to think I was a hero. I wanted you to be proud of me. All I really wanted was for you to love me." A tear rolled down his cheek. "Too late for that now."

He took the gun he'd taken from Jeffery's apartment out of his pocket.

CHAPTER 48: SHAY

July 1, 2022: 11:36 a.m.

Both men saw the blood trail turn toward the forest. Winslow reached out and grabbed Shay's arm as he was about to follow the trail off the road.

"No," Doyle said.

Shay gave Doyle an angry look. Somehow, he felt Lori was his responsibility. Why, he didn't know. Okay, he'd helped her. And, she'd helped him rescue Harper. But for the most part, he barely knew the woman.

"Victor could be in there with her," the deputy continued, "He has had time to catch up. He could use her as a hostage, and we don't know if he's armed.

"And I'm wearing a vest," Winslow added. "So, I'll go first. Stay behind me."

Shay was not happy, but he nodded. What Doyle was saying made sense. He wondered if Winslow could see how worried he was.

They hadn't gone far into the woods when Winslow held up his hand. He was standing by a large blow-down. The green tree was still alive and had come down recently. Its green boughs billowed out not far to Shay's left.

Winslow waved him close and pointed down.

Shay gasped, stepped over the log, and knelt. A shirt had been tied to Lori's side. She was breathing, but her breathing seemed strained. Blood had soaked into the shirt.

"And I have a signal," Winslow said.

Shay looked up and saw the deputy smile as he looked at

his cell phone.

After Doyle had called in an airlift to land in the meadow they'd left not that long before, Doyle looked at Shay. "The helicopter is on a life flight taking an injured fisherman to St. Pat's in Missoula. It will be about forty minutes before it can get here. The helicopter will still be able to get Lori to the hospital before we'd be able to by car.

"Can you run back and get your truck? We can lay her down in the bed and take her to the meadow."

.

Shay pulled up to the spot where Lori's blood trail entered the woods and began to turn around. Winslow stepped out of the trees on the opposite side of the road. Shay realized he'd been hiding, hoping Victor would come back. He felt a flash of anger at the idea of Lori being bait but realized Doyle hadn't put her in that situation. And his anger told him something about himself. He had feelings for her.

Winslow lifted Lori as gently as he could and carried her to the truck.

Lowering the tailgate, Shay jumped up and helped Winslow slide her into the center of the truck bed. She groaned as Shay eased her down with her head in his lap.

Her eyes opened a bit and Shay smiled at her. "It's going to be okay," he whispered.

He looked toward Winslow, who was eyeing the forest again from the side of the truck.

"What about Victor?" Shay asked.

Doyle looked at him. The deputy thought for a moment, then took out his phone.

.

"The helicopter is still twenty minutes out," Winslow said as he ended the call. "A team of deputies and highway patrol are on their way to help me look for Victor. They should be here soon."

.

Shay moved so he was leaning against the side of the truck bed with Lori's head in his lap. He took Lori's hand in his and held it.

Winslow seemed antsy. "Will you be okay to stay here alone with her for a few minutes? I can do a little tracking and see if I can figure out which way he's gone. That way they'll have an idea where to look when backup gets here.

Shay nodded and watched Winslow walk off into the forest, studying the ground but looking up every few seconds or so to keep watch around him. In minutes, the deputy vanished from sight.

"Hey," Lori said.

Shay looked down and his heart lifted. Lori's eyes were open, and she was smiling.

"Hey, yourself."

"I'm sorry I'm so much trouble," Lori said, reaching out and touching his arm with her free hand.

"Trouble," Shay said, exaggerating the word. "Lady, you don't know what trouble is."

It was then that something hit him hard on the back of the head.

A wave of blackness washed over him. He was stunned, but he did not lose consciousness. He saw Victor's braced-leg swing over the side of the truck. An instant later Victor was in.

The next instant, he felt his revolver being pulled from his holster. He caught sight of it sailing over the side of the truck. Then, strong arms lifted him under his arms. He watched helplessly as Lori's head fell off his lap and bounced against the floor of the truck.

"Damn meddling asshole." Victor cried. "I'm going to kill you with my bare hands."

Shay knew he had to act. The man was probably going to throw him out of the truck. His head already hurt, and a fall might knock him out. He'd be helpless against this guy who wanted to kill him.

"Victor! No Victor! Don't hurt him," Lori called out.

For a moment, the hands holding him loosened their grip. Shay used all his strength to push himself to his feet and twist around at the same time.

Victor's angry eyes bore into his as Shay threw a punch. All the fear Shay ever felt filled him at that moment. He wanted to be somewhere else. Anywhere else. But he couldn't be. There was going to be a fight and this time he had to win. But Shay was no fighter and his punch glanced off Victor's cheek.

As quickly as he could, Shay kicked out, aiming between Victor's legs. Victor doubled over, pushing Shay away as he did so.

But then, a small revolver appeared in Victor's right hand. The gun was coming up and Shay knew—in an instant it would be pointed right at him.

Shay kicked out again with his right leg. Out of sheer luck, his knee connected with Victor's gun hand and the gun went flying off into the brush. An instant later, Victor grabbed Shay's shoulder and pushed him out of the truck. Shay hit the ground hard. The impact knocking his breath out of him. Victor swung down and grabbed Shay by the throat.

Victor was stronger than he was. Try as he might, Shay couldn't break the man's grip on his throat. Darkness began to close in about his vision. All Shay could see was Victor's angry eyes.

CHAPTER 49: LORI

July 1, 2022: 12:16 p.m.

Lori had only glimpsed something moving behind Shay's head before Shay was suddenly collapsing. An instant later, Victor had somehow gotten into the truck, and he was lifting Shay to his feet. Her head slipped off Shay's lap and hit the truck bed hard.

Then she heard Victor's voice, say, "Damn meddling asshole. I'm going to kill you with my bare hands."

"Victor! No! Don't hurt him," she cried out, trying to stand.

Her legs were wobbly. She began to lift herself but fell to her knees. She tried again.

Victor cried out in pain. She turned to see Victor push Shay over the side and jump down after him...

Lori searched frantically for a weapon. Then she saw the walking stick she'd used in their search for Harper. It was still in the truck. But it had rolled against the other side of the truck away from her. Crawling on her knees, she crossed the truck bed and grabbed the stick.

Try as she might, she found she could not stand. She turned onto her back and using her legs and arms slid over to the tailgate.

The drop to the ground sent a wash of pain and nausea through her. But she had landed on her legs.

Hurry, she told herself. But all she could do was move in slow motion.

As she rounded the back of the truck, she could see that Shay's face was turning blue. Victor was crushing down on the man's throat with all the strength he had.

Letting go of the truck, she swung the walking stick. It landed on the top of Victor's head. Victor seemed to deflate like a balloon.

She fell on top of him.

Lori moved off Victor, then struggled to roll Victor off Shay.

It seemed to take forever for Shay's eyes to focus. Shay looked at her. After a minute, he forced a smile.

"Are you okay?" she asked.

"I will be when we get this guy tied up," Shay said, trying to rise. "Good thing we bought all that rope."

She was back in the truck bed, when Winslow came back.

"I thought I'd better come back. I didn't find any sign of him going upstream," Winslow said.

"That's cause he's in the truck," Shay said.

Lori would never forget Winslow's expression as he peered over the side of the truck. His eyes went to the tightly bound figure lying unconscious beside her.

"Well, I'll be," Winslow said. His eyes then met Lori's. "How are you doing?"

"I've been better," she said.

CHAPTER 50: SHAY

July 2, 4:12 p.m.

Shay was sitting in Lori Mysek's private hospital room Saturday afternoon when Winslow Doyle walked in.

.

Shay had spent Friday afternoon and the early part of the evening in the waiting room while Lori was in surgery. He had ridden in with her on the helicopter. Because he said he was her husband, they let him stay with her in her room overnight.

When he called Issy in the morning, he wasn't surprised that Issy had everything running smoothly.

"Buy some flowers for her room," Issy insisted.

It occurred to Shay, then, that women did seem to have quite a bit of control in his life. But he bought a bouquet in the hospital gift shop and found Lori awake when he arrived back to the room.

"Wow," was all she said, taking in the rather large bouquet he had purchased.

There was a look in her eyes that he couldn't quite read.

And all he could do was smile.

.

Now, Lori looked to Winslow expectantly.

"Well," Winslow said. "Since Victor was on parole, he has gone right back to prison. He'll wait there for trial, and he may face the death penalty for murdering Jeffery Boothe."

Shay watched a tear roll down Lori's cheek. He assumed this time the tears were for Jeffery. She wiped her eyes after a moment and seemed to pull herself together.

It was the second time she'd cried that day. Shay had been there when the doctor had told her, that she was not pregnant.

The doctor explained there were numerous reasons why a false positive, on a pregnancy test, though rare, might occur. But the bottom line was she had never been pregnant.

"You're both young. There's no reason you can't try again," the doctor said before leaving.

Lori's mouth fell open as the doctor left.

"I had to tell him we were married, so I could stay with you," Shay said.

New tears rolled down Lori's cheek. He didn't know whether it was for Jeffery Boothe, or not actually being pregnant, or for everything, or something else altogether.

"You both were really lucky," Winslow said. They both looked at him. The deputy seemed to hesitate.

"But then," he continued, "the way you rescued that treasure hunter makes me think that maybe it might not be all luck in your case.

"So." Winslow hesitated only for an instant and then continued. "I saw the private investigator certificate in your office, Mr. Hamilton," Winslow said, looking at Shay. "And," he turned to Lori. "I saw yours on the lawn outside your apartment. I guess Victor threw it there. Anyway, neither of you are licensed."

"I don't think you can actually say we were working as private investigators when we found Harper," Lori said quickly.

Winslow laughed and smiled at her. "I am not looking to charge you with working as private investigators without a license, if that's what you are thinking.

"Instead, I have a proposition. You two seem to have some natural skills. Skills that perhaps I could use. You see, I'm a part-time deputy and I also have a Private Investigation license. My background as an MP in the military qualified me even without my experience as a deputy.

"What I am proposing is, if it suits you, would either of

you, or both of you, be willing to work under my license as a private investigator? Because, I'd be happy to have you."

A big smile crossed Lori's face. She looked at Shay. She could tell by the look on his face that he was as interested as she was.

"You would both have to pay a hefty application fee. Which will be more if you include firearms under your license. And you will have to take a test. But I'm pretty sure you'd both pass with flying colors. What do you say?"

--The End—

If you enjoyed this book please leave a review. And if you haven't read them, check out the two previous Winslow Doyle Mysteries.

Winslow: The Lost Hunters

David Francis Curran

Winslow: The Lost Hunters

Winslow Doyle is a former MP and Marine Sniper. He has been a recluse living in the wilderness since his wife died some years ago, supporting himself by cutting firewood and finding lost dogs. When a desperate mother asks him to find her husband and teenage daughter, missing since the opening day of hunting season, Winslow agrees. It is a decision that will change his life.

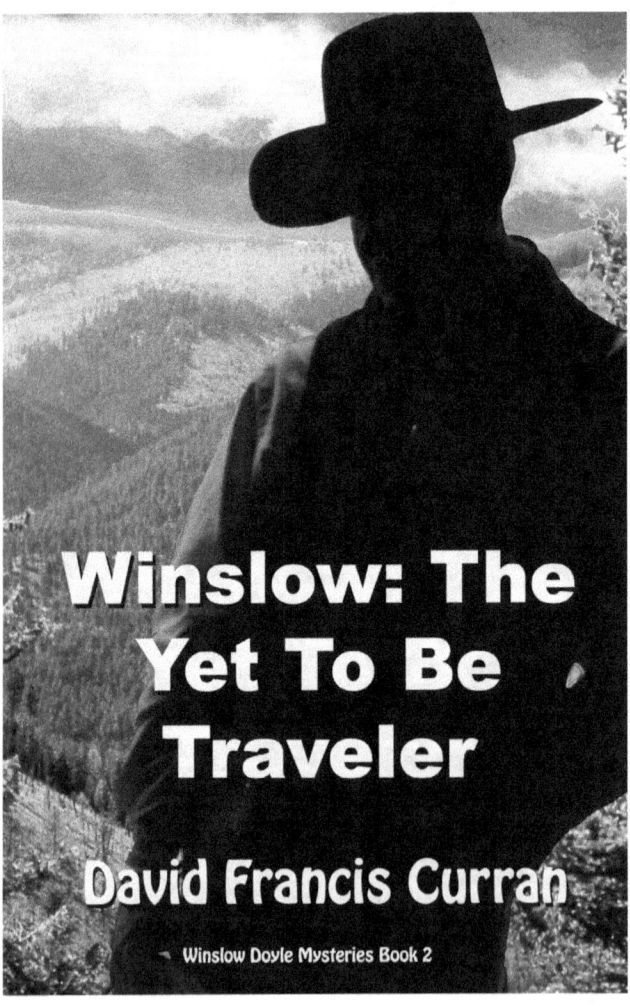

Winslow: The Yet to be Traveler

Winslow uncovers one of the biggest big store cons ever conceived. And saves the life of a young woman by doing so.

ACKNOWLEDGMENTS

I want to thank my wife and life-long editor, Patricia, for helping me develop my characters.

I want to thank publication editors Kaylie Burchfield and Ann Attwood for getting the story in shape.

And the very talented audible narrator for this book, Melissa Irish.

I would also like to thank three Udemy.com instructors for inspiration.

Eugene Matthews for introducing me to timeline analysis.

Mike Foley, whose course on the basics of fiction writing was a comfort while I ate breakfast.

And the inspirational Marissa Burt, whose HOW TO WRITE AND PUBLISH A NOVEL is something I wish I could have taken before starting my first novel years ago. I recommend her course to anyone trying to write a novel, whether it be a first or whatever. When you have finished Marissa's course, you will miss listening to her lessons in the morning before starting your writing day.

www.ingramcontent.com/pod-product-compliance
Lightning Source LLC
Chambersburg PA
CBHW051239170626
46809CB00004B/1399